Bigfoot is a Teenager

Author

Chelsea Songbird

Bigfoot Is A Teenager

The characters and the story in this book are fiction.

www.chelseasongbird.com

Copyright© 2012 by **CHELSEASONGBIRD PUBLISHING CO.**

Library of Congress Control Number: 2013902731

ISBN 978-0-9846217-2-9

Forward

Even though this is a fictional novel, it doesn't mean Bigfoot is not real. There have been many sightings all over the world. All these people cannot be wrong.

Bigfoot is a distant relative of the human being, whether he is smarter, or his senses are stronger is a mystery to all who have been seeking out his presence. He has never been caught but has been seen by many. You decide who is smarter.

I want to dedicate this book to all organizations whose goal is to add value and morals to every young girls life so they can grow to be responsible women.

Introduction

Bigfoot has many names, but all agree on one thing, he is very big. The people who have spotted a Bigfoot have life changing thoughts about mankind. When they tell their story about there sighting, they do so with great enthusiasm. They feel special in a world of very ordinary people compared to what a Bigfoot's life would be. You see they can relate to a Bigfoot's life-style because they have no doubt about their existence. In order for Bigfoot to exist he must have a family, to keep the race from becoming extinct. We all know that teenage years are very different than any other time in life for human beings. This holds true for the teenage Bigfoot as well. What we have in this book is a chance taking teenage Bigfoot. Bigfoot is the typical teenager.

www.chelseasongbird.com

Table of Contents

Chapter 1

Scottie's Encounter

"It was a warm summer afternoon when Scottie went down to the creek to play near the water. He enjoyed skimming rocks across a stream of water that is approximately 20 feet wide. The stream is slow moving and Scottie is an excellent swimmer so his parents give him the freedom to play where he wants as long as he doesn't venture to far from home. On this particular afternoon Scottie was looking into the water at his reflection, when suddenly he seen two large glowing green reflections in the water. Scottie's eyes were not sure if what he was looking at is something at the bottom of the stream or a reflection from an overhanging tree, with brightly colored leaves. He put his hand into the water to pick up what he thought was a shinny glowing green rock when suddenly he realized what he was seeing was not on the bottom of the stream but was coming from above. As the water moved from Scottie putting his hand into it, the reflection of a large figure with reddish tent moved. He than knew it was something hovering above him. His body became frozen with fear for this thing is monstrous, deviating greatly from the norm in structure or appearance, and its abnormal in size. The glowing green reflections disappear for a moment and than reappear. Scottie realized the red figure behind him just blinked its eyes. Chill's filled Scottie's body and the hair on the back of his neck stood up. A foul smell filled the air as Scottie realized this thing hovering over him could

1

feel the fear in Scottie's body. It could sense Scottie is aware of its presence and suddenly it leaps across the twenty-foot stream and only one foot touches the water. Scottie is shaken by the enormous humanoid covered in red hair. Everything becomes quite, not a sound, its as if the only movement is the breath coming out of Scotties lungs. The ground, which is covered with a mat of mosses and the broad-leafed trees that let in only a small amount of sunlight made it impossible for Scottie to tell which direction the Wildman took. It's as if the glowing green eyes hypnotized Scottie for it was some time before he was able to move. A high-pitched squealing noise from the creature broke the spell and Scottie turned and ran to his house screaming all the way. By the time he finally made it to his mothers arms he was shaking and crying uncontrollable. Scottie's mother took him to the hospital, where he was given medication to calm him down.

This gentlemen, is what brings us together today. We need to get to the bottom of Scottie's story," said Professor Sprinkle.

Crystal looked at me and said, "Chelsea, what do you think Scottie seen." I shrugged my shoulders and said, "I haven't a clue. I'm just here to sell my Diva Girl cookies like you should be doing. We are getting off track as to why we came in this restaurant in the first place.

This thing they are talking about isn't any of our business. Do you think any of those guys would want to buy some cookies?"

We went about our business, going booth, to booth, selling Diva Girl cookies when one of the men from the private dinning room waved us over and asked, "Do you have any chocolate mint cookies, and could I buy a box?" I handed him a box and he held it up and told everyone in the room that he had heard Bigfoot liked chocolate mint cookies. They all got a chuckle out of that and we sold all our cookies. There must have been twenty-five people listening to that man talk about Scottie's experience with Bigfoot. One of the many people attending this meeting offered to buy me and Crystal something to drink and said, "You girls may want to hear about what is going on in this town. Grab a chair and listen, you are out of cookies so take a break and take in some information."

We ordered a glass of tea with a slice of lemon, grabbed a chair and joined the group. Their were all kinds of people in the room, some husband and wife, some looked like trappers, a lady dressed in a suit taking notes worked for the press, she had a tag on that read, Press, Carolyn Jones. A couple of guys in the front were scientist. Others were Bigfoot enthusiast and followed all Bigfoot sightings that they could afford to attend.

The Professor began talking once again and introduced one of the scientist's that spoke next. The scientist began with some background on past sightings. He started a projector and at the top of the list is:

: The Abominable Snowman lives in the Himalayas and is also sometimes called the Yeti.
: Sasquatch lives in Canada.
: Wildman species lives in the Russian mountains.
: Bigfoot lives in Oklahoma, California, Oregan and Washington State.
: Almas lives in Mongolia in the Tien Shan mountains.
: Orang Pendek in Indonesia.
: Shiru in Latin America.
: Muhalu in the Congo.

"As you can see the Wildman has many different names so it would be best if we could settle on one name for the Wildman and it will be Bigfoot. Most people believe the Bigfoot migrates and that is why they have been seen in so many different places. The number of people who claim to have spotted footprints in different areas, suggest migration. Most sightings are during the full moon and during drastic changes in the weather.

So much of the world is uncharted that Bigfoot could be living anywhere. The area where Scottie encountered

Bigfoot is so thick with brush I doubt any civilized man has ever stepped on the ground where Bigfoot vanished before Scottie's eyes. The moon is still full and that should help with finding Bigfoot. I see some of you are carrying guns, which is fine, I want you to keep in mind that Bigfoot is not a monster and unless you feel your life is in danger, do not shoot him. If Bigfoot is shot in the back you will go on trial for shooting a human being. In other words, you can't hunt down Bigfoot, and kill a Bigfoot for he is a giant human being. On the other hand, if Bigfoot is stalking you and attacks you, protection of one's self is allowed. No Bigfoot has ever been seen any way other than running away until Scottie's sighting. Is that clear enough? With that I want to turn over the spotlight to Dr. Ben Holt, he is a scientist in Paleoanthropology, which is the search for human origins, and Cryptozoology which is the study of hidden animals, and Paleontology which is the study of animals lost in time. You may never get another chance to visit with such a highly educated man in your life so take advantage of it and pick his brain. Let's give Dr. Ben Holt a big welcome," said Dr. James Niles.

"Thank you, Thank you, you can be seated now. I want to bring you up to date on what concrete facts we have gathered since Scottie's encounter with Bigfoot. We found prints on some boulders near where Scottie seen Bigfoot, and brought in an expert in Dermatoglyphs, which is finger printing, to diagnose the findings. The three-inch long fingerprints we found are definitely human, only quite large. The swirls of ridges on the palms indicate this human is rather young. Further up the trail we found where Bigfoot had a bowl movement, and he buried it. This may be why evidence of his existence has been so hard to find. In the floor of the forest things degrade very rapidly. We think Scottie scared the 'you know what' out of Bigfoot and he got careless by not shoving leaves and moss over his fresh dirt. Ten pounds of dung was removed and it definitely is human. There is one difference, no parasites were found in the dung, and this could account for the size and agility of Bigfoot. He could very well be the healthiest human on earth.

No longer is the lack of scientific respect, for sightings of a Bigfoot, part of our scientific world. Global warming has brought Bigfoot out of the hills and mountains, into the lowlands, where very well respected people all over the world have reported seeing Bigfoot. Science is backing up the fact that he is human with DNA testing of anything Bigfoot leaves behind.

I'm currently studying Bigfoot's migration patterns. Bigfoot is more than just a possibility and I want to be the one to confirm his existence. The gargantuan footprint is not made by any ordinary human being, it comes from a super human. This is a Plaster of Paris footprint taken from the other side of the stream where Scottie had his encounter with Bigfoot. It is 20 inches long and six inches wide. My friends this is truly a Bigfoot.

Bigfoot recently has been sighted in Japan, Russia and France. Anthropologists all over the world are teaming up with biologists to find this human ancestor. Many will be joining us before the week is out.

The way Scottie described Bigfoot's whistle is very much the same as most people have described it over many years. The sound is shrill and distorted. Nothing like Scottie has ever heard. We believe the tone has hidden messages for other Bigfoot's, warnings or something like that. Much like whale's talk to each other with high tones, low tones, and in between tones. This is how everyone describes the whistle from Bigfoot.

Tracks were found in Oregon last week. A group of anthropological and zoological experts are analyzing the findings on Pine Ridge and coming up with the same things we are today. This may suggest many tribes of Bigfoot exist.

I recently went on an expedition in the Himalayas where the low-oxygen environment high in the mountains made everyone feel limp, like their muscles lost their power. Across the mountain, an avalanche occurred just from the sound of a mountaineer hollering out his location. As we watched the avalanche take down the side of the mountain, a white figure, what looked to be 20 feet tall hurried out of the way. It was not limp or woozy like we were from all the altitude up high, it was fast and strong, like what we believe Bigfoot to be.

We are taking our rifles to protect ourselves from bears and large cats. Bigfoot is a human, just like us and unless he attacks you and your life is in danger, he is off limits. Each of you will be issued a knife for protection, don't use it unless you fear for your life," said Dr. Holt.

Professor Sprinkle took the stage once again to introduce a young Japanese boy by the name of Kale. The boy flew into the United States with his parents a month ago and they were staying in Oregon where another sighting of a red haired Bigfoot took place. He arrived in Oklahoma early this morning after hearing about Scottie's sighting. Kale wanted to talk to someone young like himself, who had an encounter with a green eyed red haired Bigfoot, as he did in Japan.

"I would now like to introduce Kale Taira who is fourteen years old and lives in a small city called Beppu in Japan. He also has encountered a red haired Bigfoot in Japan. Let's give him a warm welcome," said Professor Sprinkle. Everyone in the room got up out of their chairs and began clapping their hands. All were filled with excitement to hear the details of Kale's encounter.

"Thank you very much for the warm welcome. I'm very excited to share my story with all of you. I spent time with Scottie early this morning and he describes his sighting of Bigfoot very similar to my own. I would like to begin with some information about earthquakes in my country, Japan. It is legend that Japan is the back of a huge, sleeping sea dragon. The earthquakes are caused when the sleeping sea dragon wakes up. Japan is made up of many islands and on the island of Honshu is Mt. Fuji, Japan's highest mountain and is believed to be the home of Bigfoot. Mt. Fuji is sixty-two miles from Tokyo and is 12,388 feet high, and it is a dormant volcano. Mt. Fuji is a majestic snow capped mountain with a picturesque aqua Pacific Ocean coastline. Mt. Fuji last erupted in 1707.

Another volcano, called Mt. Unzen, erupted in 1782 and created waves in the ocean that killed 10,000 people. The waves, called tsunamis, are created from an avalanche of the volcano dropping into the ocean. Right before the tsunamis, the ocean water becomes white, frozen in place like a mirror reflecting the clouds. Then the rumbling becomes closer and closer with powerful tremors that are being felt continuously.

When a volcano erupts the earth begins shifting in different directions and smoke rises majestically from the womb of the world, only to give birth to a new island. Volcanoes bring fertile volcanic soil to the surface from the inside of the earth, to give earth new life. Other planets that are dead; have dead volcano's inside of them. This tells you that volcano's erupting is necessary for our planet to be alive. We have the only planet that has plate movement, and is alive. All the rest of the planets are either hotter or frozen and dead, with no plate movement. A lot of lives have been lost due to the volcano's, but without them, none of us would be alive for long.

Indonesia had more volcanic activity than any place on earth, and is actually made up of volcanoes. There are twenty-one active volcanoes on the island of Java. Krakatoa is only six degrees south of the equator and erupted on May 25, 1883. On July 30th 1883 Krakatoa blasted lava from the center of the earth until it became level. The tectonic plates below Java caused the eruption due to subterranean shifting. It lasted for twenty hours and fifty-six minutes. It was a traumatizing event. The sound from the eruption is extraordinary loud. The explosion is like a roar coming out of the crater with white steam in the beginning and later turning to black with gray ash. The air was filled with an unusual darkness as the ash cascaded out of the plumes of smoke. The air was filled with vibrations as the falling ash, rich in iron, filled the air. The iron in the ash made the compasses spin out of control, leaving people without direction.

As the sun set it took on a soft white glow as the clouds passed before it like ribbons floating in the sky. The full moon became a looming silhouette of incredible beauty that came and went through the night as the clouds of ash rolled across the sky.

It is said that above Krakatoa was a burning red fiery blaze. As the mountain was intensifying it's activity and gathering power, the tremors became stronger. It was a fearful sight. It is said that the volcanic cloud rose seventeen miles above Krakatoa. It was raining rocks on fire and lightning strikes were the only light to be seen in the pumice ash that filled the eerily dark sky. The last explosion was the loudest ever recorded even to this day. It was heard thousands of miles away. It is believed to have thrown rocks twenty-four miles into the sky. Many thought it to be the end of the world. Windows began to shatter from the high frequency sound that broke the silence followed by a gigantic explosion. The town of Ketimbang was flooded and totally destroyed by water. An old man and his family were in a boat and survived to tell what happened to his home in Ketimbang and asked that his story live forever in his offspring. This is how we know so much about the volcano, he was a eye witness to the event.

He told how a wave of considerable height has caused some of the small islands to completely disappear while new islands never seen before have emerged from the water. The eruption destroyed 165 villages and killed 36,417 people. Most died from sea water, and few actually died from being covered with hot ash, burning cinders, and burning lava. Some died from sulfur-dioxide gas that was released during the eruption, which is poison, and suffocates them.

Krakatoa caused two giant waves, like a wall of water so gigantic and full of force it washed people off the earth with its erratic motion. Those on ships, like the old man, were safer than those on land, with a ship you had a chance of ridding the wave, on land you had no chance. It was as if the water was restless with a low-frequency pulsation, the sea was moving north and south at the same time. It was a terrifying and unimaginable destructive wall of water. The high-frequency noises traveled at 675 miles per hour. The giant wall of water went from green to black. The forth shock wave of Krakatoa circled the world seven times. It had reverberated and the barographs all over the world recorded the shock wave of Krakatoa. The island of Dwaisindeweg was split into five different islands and sixteen new volcanic islands were formed. Krakatoa disappeared into the sea, gone forever.

The glowing vapors made the sun look alive and green in some parts of the world, and to an orange and red glow in other parts of the world. Six weeks after Krakatoa's eruption, ash had reached half way across the world. The earth became cold and dark. It was unnerving, the chill in the air with the purple and red sky had some thinking it was the end of time.

The half-mile high Krakatoa was blown off the face of the earth, half blown into the sky and the other half dropped into the ocean. Ships could no longer use Krakatoa as a landmark for traveling between Java and Sumatra. The mineral pumice floats on water and many of the trees on Krakatoa had this pumice entangled in their roots allowing them to float for thousands of miles.

The eruption in 1815 of Tambora in Indonesian ejected eleven cubic miles of debris into the atmosphere, twice as much as Krakatoa.

The year of 1816 was declared the year without a summer. The largest volcano ever to erupt is Mount Toba, in northern Sumatra, 74,000 years ago. It left behind a lake fifty miles long and fifteen miles wide.

Fish, poultry, and animals are sensitive to weather, volcano, and internal earth movement. Fish that normally live at the bottom of the ocean come to the surface. Animals vacate an area where an earthquake takes place. Hens stop laying eggs. They do all this before mankind can even register this on machines.

Last week I visited Mount St. Helen, which exploded in May 1980. It was the home of many Bigfoot sightings. I'm sure that Bigfoot left this Mount St. Helen before it erupted and that is why there are so many sightings all over America. The Bigfoot family had to relocate when they felt the earth rumbling under their feet.

I had to share my knowledge about volcano's and earthquakes because they are the cause for the migration of Bigfoot across the entire world in my opinion. My research is proving a direct link to Bigfoot and plates shifting under the earth.

In Japan I live in a small city called Beppu. It is famous for its hot springs, which are created by the movement of the Earth's plates. The pools of water are heated from deep inside the earth. I have my very own hot-spring spa in my back yard. Beppu also has a forest that adds to the beauty of this small city.

Japan has 127 million citizens. The Japanese people call their country Nippon. The sun is an important symbol in Japan. The sun represents the red circle on the Japanese national flag. Now that you know about my studies of earthquakes and volcano's and a little about where I live, it's time to give you a detailed account of my personal encounter with Bigfoot.

I practice the art of sword yoga. It makes yoga more exciting when I wale my father's sword while stretching my muscles. The sword is a symbol of the Japanese character and manhood rather than as a mere tool. It gives me pride to practice safe handling of my father's sword. He has dulled the edge so I can't hurt myself, and the blade of the sword shines like a mirror. This is how I first seen Bigfoot.

I was stretching with the sword above my head, when the reflection of two green glowing eyes, were on the sword. I froze in place upon the sight of these glowing eyes. I watched the pupils grow larger when the creature realized I was aware of his presence. We were eye to eye even though he was behind me. As his pupils became larger a foul smell filled the air. I'm not sure if the smell was because of fear or was it meant as an intimidation. Whatever the case, we were eye to eye through the reflection of the sword. Bigfoot blinked and when he did I turned to face him. I turned, and so did he, and off he went into the trees. I ran behind him hollering, 'wait, wait, I won't hurt you.' I dropped my dad's sword and continued to follow Bigfoot. He was not really trying to escape me for he has a stride that could leave me in the dust. He was toying with me, wanting me to chase him. He wouldn't allow me to get close enough to see his entire body. He was always half covered by brush or was halfway hid behind the trunk of a tree. It was like a game to him. He was having fun with me. In my opinion, the Bigfoot that I encountered is a teenager like myself. This Bigfoot cannot control his impulse to toy with me. He is risking his secret life to play hiding seek. You see the frontal lobes are the last part of the brain to develop according to the National Institute of Mental Health, and continues to develop in our twenty's. If teens would just ask themselves, 'what are the long-term consequences of what I'm about to do,' then their decisions may be different. No adult Bigfoot would ever toy with a human, for fear that they, the human, would find his home, and expose them to the world. This teenage Bigfoot was being reckless and if his parents were aware of his actions I'm sure he would be put in timeout.

As I ran toward Bigfoot, suddenly he turned and he was heading in my direction. I froze like an ice cube, unable to move. All I could think about is why did I drop my dad's sword. I could use it to protect myself or to scare away the Bigfoot. I try to move my foot but I'm totally immobile, unable to even blink my eyes. Bigfoot is coming closer and closer. His hair is as red as blood and the glow from his green eyes is blinding. He looks to be ten feet tall. As he stands in front of me his pupils grow larger and larger until the green glow becomes black. His red hair is standing on end. Its as if he has total control over every hair on his body. He squeals out a high-pitched noise that was deafening, and breathes a foul smell in my face, and turns to scurry up the side of the hill. His stride was as long as he is tall. He was completely out of sight within a moment. I no longer had any desire to chase him. As my body regained flexibility I melted to the ground with great fear. It was as if my muscles were mush. Tears were falling from my eyes but I was not sobbing. The tears were just flowing uncontrollable. I sat on the ground for some time digesting what just happened to me. My emotions were jumping from fear to joy of what I just experienced. I felt special to have witnessed the reality that Bigfoot does exist.

As I gather myself together and wiped the wetness from my face, I realized I just experienced what many people have been chasing all their life. You see, in Japan, we are aware of the existence of Bigfoot, and hold him in high esteem. We know he is real.

That summer day my parents were at work, I stayed by myself, seeing how I am now fourteen years old, I did not need anyone looking after me. The neighbors are retired and if I ever needed anything they would be who I would go to. What I just experienced would first be shared with my parents. I would just wait until they got home from work. My heart was busting with joy as I relived what had just happened to me. Walking through the woods and glancing over my shoulder to see if I could get another glimpse of Bigfoot, I realized my life would never be the same. I would always want another encounter with this magnificent giant of a man.

I picked up my fathers sword and headed for the hot springs. I leaned the sword against a tree hoping for another reflection of Bigfoot as I stepped into the warm water and sank my body up to my chin. The water took away all the tension Bigfoot had created. I looked up to the sky and just relived the experience over and over in my mind.

I'm here today to join each of you in the hunt to once again get a glance of Bigfoot. I know I will be chasing him for my entire life. That's the kind of impact he has made on me," said Kale.

The entire room stood up and clapped their hands for Kale and the story he told. He bowed his head in acknowledgement of the gratitude of the group. It had everyone in the room thinking about what their reaction would be if they came face to face with Bigfoot. Would they be able to just drink in his presence or would they be fear-stricken. No one knows what they will do until the situation presents itself to them. It has to be in your face before you know what you will do.

I was spooked by what I had seen and heard and looked at Crystal like what did we just sit through? Crystal had the same look on her face and she said, "I think we should be getting back to camp. You know Chelsea Songbird that Bigfoot has never hurt anybody that they can prove. Everything that I've ever heard about the big guy is that he just wants to be left alone. When he sees people he high tails it out to higher land."

Crystal has a point, Bigfoot, the hairy guy, is a phenomenon in the fact he has yet to be captured and the legend lives, does he exist or not? Is he the imagination of a lot of different people or is he real? I believe Bigfoot possessed instinct lost to humans, do to our civil raising. I think he is one of our ancestors who has not been subjected to civilization. No one has ever proved that Bigfoot hurt anybody. Everyone who has seen him has chased him. I think it's okay that he is untamed, unlike the rest of us with our languages and set of rules to follow. Bigfoot does what he wants all day long and whistles at the other Bigfoot people when he wants company.

Anthropological views dismiss Bigfoot as a hoax, because there are no bones to examine, he is viewed as a superstition of the wild imagination of those who need drama in their lives. The way they were talking in the restaurant about Bigfoot, you would think he is revered and respected. I'm on the side of the believer.

Chapter 2

Climbing Tiger Mountain

Our Diva Girls leader, Jan, called a meeting to say thanks for the great job everyone did selling the cookies and candy bars. The proceeds will be donated to gifted individuals, for higher education programs.

"As you all know, we met our goals. The revenue will make a great difference in the family's life that we are sponsoring in the higher education program. The girls name is Zoe and she will be able to start her higher math class with a tutor, a private instructor this summer.

Zoe will be on her way to becoming a scientist, and thanks to each of you, she will have the opportunity to finish college early and start her research to cure the diseases that plague the world. Zoe is only 10 years old but her ability for math is years beyond her age. Her school has no one to teach her the level of mathematics that she tested for, college, in the second year. With our help, by the time Zoe is 16 years old she will be working with other scientist.

Each of you can take Diva pride in the fact that we are helping Zoe reach her full potential at an early age. Who knows, she may be the very one to find a cure for a disease that has plagued mankind with a great affliction full of pain and suffering since the beginning of time. It would make my heart sing to have a hand in making a dreaded disease disappear from the face of the earth. I hope each of you feel deeply about your hands on gift you are giving to Zoe.

All of you are part of making this world a better place to live by helping the girls who are gifted with intelligence, push their self to the max with tutors, which they could never afford without your help.

Intelligence is a gift from God and we are helping those with a gift reach their full potential. This puts a smile on God's face. You can all give yourself a pat on the back for a job well done," Jan said.

The Diva Girls had a great time selling the cookies and candy bars while at the same time they gained experience in marketing and sales. It was a winning situation for all.

Bigfoot is on my mind right now. All the attention he is getting in town let's me know he had a lot of followers. This tells me he is not just a myth, he exist. The boys, Scottie, and Kale, describe Bigfoot just like all the other people who have seen him only their Bigfoot has red hair. I totally understand the fear that pierced Scotties body when he realized the green things in the water weren't rocks, but were the glowing eyes of Bigfoot who was standing right behind him. I probably would have fainted and fell face down in the water, which would wake me up, but I would have missed Bigfoot running into the woods like what Scottie seen. When Kale seen Bigfoot in the blade of the sword and turned to chase Bigfoot into the woods, I probably would have dropped the sword, ran into the house, locked the door, and called my parents.

No one knows what he or she might do unless the situation actually happened to him or her. I'm not one to put myself in a dangerous situation. Everything I know about Bigfoot is that he just wants his space. When people invade his space he has been know to throw rocks at them, but he has never hit them with a rock. He has however hit trucks and tents with rocks.

The two week camping trip with the Diva Girls is exciting enough, but now that Bigfoot is on Tiger Mountain the trip is being bumped up a notch or two.

It's evening and I'm standing at the base of Tiger Mountain

looking up to the top when the leader of our group, Jan, approached me and said, "How are you doing Chelsea." I replied, "Just fine. I was looking at how high this mountain is and was wondering how high up will the Diva Girls be going in the morning." Jan pointed to a bluff that looked to be half way up the mountain, "Right about there, where that flat spot is, about half way up Tiger Mountain. You will be able to see for miles and miles from that spot. It's breathtaking," said Jan.

As I gaze upon the spot Jan pointed to, excitement filled my senses. It is like a rush of adventure just filled my body. Exploring new places always stimulates my mind.

"Jan, there is a lot of talk about Bigfoot living on Tiger Mountain, and the boy Scottie coming face to face with him, do you think there is much of a chance we will run into him while we are hiking in his home?" I said.

"Chelsea, that very question has crossed my mind. You know first of all, Bigfoot was spotted 10 miles from here on the other side of where we are going. It is highly unlikely he will be in the same area that the Diva Girls will be going and besides that the Guy Troops are already up there and no one from that organization has reported seeing any Bigfoot's. If it will make you feel any better a forest ranger will be escorting us. All of the people searching for Bigfoot will be going up Tiger mountain from the spot where Scottie seen Bigfoot. That is a long way from where we are hiking." Jan said.

As I gazed across Tiger Mountain to the spot Jan pointed to and than back to the spot where the Diva Girls will be going, it looked like a lot of distance. However, Bigfoot has really long legs and one step for him would be like five steps for a regular person. In my mind Bigfoot could be where we are going by morning. I'm keeping those thoughts to myself. Jan is trying so hard to keep me calmed, and I don't want to ruin it for her. Besides, Bigfoot has never hurt a human being, and he only eats berries and critters. I'm sure we will all be okay.

Jan put her arm on my shoulder and we headed towards camp. It's getting late and the sun is starting to set. I look back at Tiger Mountain and the clouds are hiding the tip of the mountain. The sun has the trees looking a golden green color, one I've never seen before and I'm just drinking in the beauty of nature.

When I walked in the cabin all the Diva Girls were packing for our trip in the morning. There is a lot of talk about the brilliant little girl named Zoe that we are sponsoring. One of the girls is talking about how Jan told her about a conversation she had with Zoe. "Why would a bunch of Diva's donate money for me to get a tutor, I thought Diva's were all about their self? Do they know all their work is going for a 10 year old, girl? This means I must redefine the meaning of Diva from self consumed, to caring for humanity or do they need to be sure if they get sick I will help find a cure for whatever illness they might have. Whatever the case I'm so happy and I love the Diva Girl's for making this possible. Here I am a nerd, so different from the Diva look, yet they are taking me under their wings and lifting me up to be all I can be. This act of kindness brings me to the reality that Diva's underneath all the glam, have a heart," Zoe said, according to Jan.

I think it's good to be high on yourself, as long as you are doing the right thing. God wants us to enjoy life, and He gave every young girl, a unique personality. My personality just happened to fit in the tribe of Diva Girls. Besides, what's so wrong with us, we take a bath every day, fix our hair in a stylish way, dress to look our best and enjoy life. We are just taking care of what God gave us. I think people are just too quick to judge us because of the way we look. Belonging to the organization of the Diva Girls keeps us grounded and educates us about the joy of doing for others, which makes us whole human beings.

Crystal was already asleep and didn't even hear me say, goodnight. I could hear her snoring, guess I should get some sleep also. It's late and everyone is asleep but me. Suddenly

I hear something outside the cabin door and as I look out the window my eyes fall upon a mountain of a man, or is it a monster. Hair is covering its entire body. As it came closer to the window I seen its silhouette, an outline of an object that appears dark against a lighted background, almost like a fog taking the shape of a huge man, not a monster. The mans words in the restaurant keep ringing in my ears, "Bigfoot is more than just a legend or a myth, he is reality. Bigfoot's been seen by scientist, on Glaciers with white hair and glowing green eyes, they all testify that he is real. The creature has a long face with a wide forehead and very long arms, like a primitive human." This is exactly what I'm looking at, only instead of having the white hair he has red hair covering his entire body. The night-light is giving his red hair a glow, like extreme healthy hair has. He must be 12 feet tall. He's next to the shed now and it's at least twelve feet tall and the creature is every bit as tall. His head is turning slowly as if he can feel me looking at him. His eyes lock onto mine, glowing green and bright like nothing I've ever seen. It's as if he is looking right through me. I can't move, its like I'm paralyzed with fright. I'm looking Bigfoot right in the eye. He turns and leaps over the shed and is scurrying up the hill. The moon is full and I can see the brush being smashed to the ground as Bigfoot leaves a trail. I try to wake Crystal, she is in a deep sleep and I'm unable to wake her. Time is of most importance so I grab my backpack and flashlight and head out the door to follow the path Bigfoot is leaving. No time to waste, I must see what direction Bigfoot is taking. I had to make an ultimatum of put my fears to rest, and embellish the chance to follow Bigfoot to find where he lives, or wish I had followed him all my life. This opportunity comes only once in a lifetime.

I'm spooked as I follow the trail of broken trees limbs and grass smashed into the earth, yet I'm ecstatic about hunting Bigfoot even though the haunting fear of confronting him lingers in the back of my mind.

As I climb the hills Bigfoot blends in with the forest so

well that one moment I see him, than I lose site of him.

Suddenly I hear a whistle and there is Bigfoot on top of a rock with the moonlight heightening his image, the sound prolonged as he tilts his head back, until taken up by another ringing far away. He is not alone.

I edge closer and closer until I can see the muscles in his body flexing as he moves. The shrill noise coming from his throat heightens my fears. His head is back once again and turning in the moonlight as if he is calling to a far away place that covers the entire area that his body faces. It makes me wonder how many other's are out there that he is calling to. I hear at least two responses and then suddenly he turns and the green glowing eyes are once again locked into the core of my body and I cannot move. My mind is screaming, run, run for your life, but I'm paralyzed, lifeless, only my mind is moving and it is racing beyond control.

The foulest of smell is filling the air and I can hardly stand to take a breath. The stench is so thick I could cut it with a knife. I'm gasping for air and Bigfoot turns and leaps off the rock and is moving in the direction of the sound that responded to his high-pitched shrill whistle. The air clears of the foul smell as if he took it with him. My thoughts are that this smell is something he can turn on and off. It is like a defense mechanism to keep me at a distance. He is not a bogeyman spreading fear. He prefers to be left alone. The smell he releases is trying to tell me to get out of here. Leave me alone.

The only way I can keep following him is to keep telling myself he's not the bogeyman, I'm the bogeyman scaring him.

His size and the fact that he is so hairy, is frightening, but his green glowing eyes are what really horrify me. He knows I'm following him and when he turns to look me in the eye it is a paralyzing fear that won't let me move.

He is taking me further and further away from the cabins through brush I could never had made it through if not for him smashing it with his giant feet. The moon is so bright that I can see Bigfoot smashing the brush as he makes his way through the hills. They say Oklahoma only has hills but they feel like mountains when I'm climbing them.

Suddenly the path stops, and my flashlights light, grows dim, because of the weak batteries. I hear something in the bushes and as I turn there are those glowing green eyes for only a moment. Fear strikes my heart and my heart is now in my throat. The eyes disappear and the sound is now behind me. Cracking of dry limbs and movement in the bushes is what I rely on, for my flashlight is dim and no longer works, they are all around me now. My heart skips a beat and as I turn, there are those glowing green eyes. I think I might die any minute from fright. Could there be more than one Bigfoot in the bushes. The eyes move from one side of the bushes to the other but no sound of movement do I hear. Has the one he is calling joined Bigfoot on the hill? I start to cry, I can't hold back my fear. I'm up here by myself not even sure how to get back to the cabin and don't know if these creatures will even let me go back. I sit crying and shivering, not from cold but from fear. Exhaustion has filled my body as the glowing green eyes appear and disappear in the darkness. I pick up a stick for protection, knowing it is no match for what I'm up against, but it makes me feel better. My body is trembling from the fear and I'm becoming so weak that I melt to the ground. I think I'm dying from fear.

When I wake in the morning the sun was beaming on my face. Large footprints, at least 20 inches long are all around in the bushes where the glowing green eyes were watching me. They just left, not a hair on my head was touched.

The trail was leading deeper and deeper into the woods. Even as frightened, as I was the night before, I could not resist following these 20-inch footprints. I have to know where they are going. I know I can follow the path that Bigfoot has left to get back to the cabin, so I follow the footprints deeper into the woods. I have to know where they are going.

The ridge has movement in the bushes. I must see what the crackling is in those bushes. As I neared, the underbrush became thicker and the hill steeper. You could walk into this brush and never see a single soul. As I entered the thick trees, I felt like someone was watching me. It is the scariest feeling. I wanted so badly to just turn around and go back to the cabin, but something inside me kept pushing me forward. The trees are so dense Bigfoot could live here forever and never be spotted.

I'm nearing the bushes and the movement is slowing down. It is hard to tell if Bigfoot is psychic, or if his senses are heighten beyond the norm. If that is Bigfoot in the bushes, he knows I'm here. I can tell by the way things are getting still that it is Bigfoot making me follow this path. I slowly draw a limb of a tree back so I can get a look at what he is doing. Suddenly I'm face to face with a deer. He is frozen in time looking deep into my eyes as if to say, "what are you doing here." A smile comes across my face as I enjoy the beauty of this creature. Is this what I was feeling when the ire feeling of someone watching me came over me? This beautiful deer, I must get control of my senses.

We are staring each other down. Who will move first? Not me. Seldom does anyone get a chance to be this close to a wild animal without them scurrying off. I'm just going to look deep into these lovely big brown eyes as long as he stays here. I'm trying not to close my eyes any movement could send the deer off into the thick foliage.

Out of nowhere a huge hand grabs the deer by the neck and snaps it with a loud pop. I fall to the ground to hide myself as Bigfoot tears the deer in half. He steps on the lower half of the deer to pull it apart and begins eating it. I could hear the popping of the bones. This continues until he has devoured the entire half of the deer. The other half he threw over his neck to carry away, he is taking it to eat later.

Thoughts were going through my head, was Bigfoot using me to distract the deer? Is he what I felt was watching me? Is he as intelligent as any human being? I'm not one to give into vulnerable suggestions of irrational ideas, but I believe Bigfoot used me to distract the deer.

The foliage is so thick that anything could hide and watch your every move. Bigfoot was stalking me and the deer just happened to make a great dinner for him. I'm so hungry right now I believe I could have joined him for dinner. After all, I eat my steak rare, brown on the outside and warm in the middle. Not so very different.

The high-pitched shriek echoed through the hills as he pushed on deeper and deeper into the wilderness. A return call, with a higher tone, answered him, it must be his mate.

My legs are getting weak and I don't know if I can continue when Bigfoot stopped, lay the deer down, and began pushing a large boulder from the side of a hill. He picked the half of deer back up and entered the opening. Crawling on my hands and knees, I approached the opening and before my very eyes, Bigfoot and a female Bigfoot and two young Bigfoot's are in the cave. They are a family.

Inside what is Bigfoot's home, is a pool of water caused by a natural spring. The female is dipping a hollowed out trunk of a tree into the water as Bigfoot lay down the half of deer. The female begins to wash Bigfoot's neck and chest with leaves. Next, all four set in a circle and Bigfoot rips pieces of flesh from the deer and hands it to each of his family members. Once again I'm tempted to join them. I take out my camera and snap some shots of the family. The sun is shinning bright enough that the flash is not necessary. Only a small hole at the top of this opening of the cave is allowing the sun in, however, shiny boulders are capturing the sun's rays much like a mirror would and are reflecting the light on one another to the point it's as if they have electricity. That's how bright this dark cave is. That tiny hole by itself would only bring a small beam of light, but what Bigfoot has done with the shinny rocks is considered engineering. I'm amazed at what I'm seeing.

For me the question, "Is Bigfoot real?" has been answered. He's as real as each breath I take to fill my lungs with air. I can't see air but I know it exist.

After the family finished eating, all washed up and the

bones and dirty water were thrown over the side of the very steep hill, and Bigfoot pulled the boulder back over the entrance of their home.

"Chelsea, Chelsea, wake up. It's time for breakfast. We must hurry before the others leave us behind. The hiking begins in half an hour. We don't want to be late," Crystal said.

As I wiped the sleep from my eyes I began screaming, "I found Bigfoot, I know where he lives. I have pictures of his whole family. Let me show you." As I began pushing buttons to show the pictures, I discovered my camera was empty. Not a single picture of Bigfoot and his family. I said, "The batteries must have been low." As I continued to push buttons the camera revealed the batteries have a full charge. I continue to push buttons trying to find the pictures when Crystal said, "Chelsea you were dreaming. When I woke you, you were tossing and turning and mumbling something about family. You had a dream."

I opened the cabin door to look outside to see where I was. I've never had such a real dream if that is what happened. I looked at the 12-foot shed where I first saw the Bigfoot, and he was every bit as tall as that shed. I just don't know how a dream could seem so real.

With time I realized indeed it was a dream. This will be one dream I will never forget, it had me questioning weather it really happened or not, I actually could not tell at first.

I filled my plate with beacon, eggs, toast with jelly and grabbed a cup of grape juice. I'm very hungry just like in the dream. Bigfoot is the topic at the breakfast table as I go back for some more eggs.

Chapter 3

Hiking Expedition

The Diva leader started the day with a check of all the necessary staples for our hiking expedition. In our backpacks we have water, food, first aid kits, raincoats and bug spray. We leave at daybreak and return the next day. This particular trip we are looking for the blue butterfly that resides way up the hillside in a meadow full of bluebell flowers. It's three miles, uphill all the way. We have our cameras charged so we can document our findings, and also turn them into pieces of artwork. On the day after we return from our hiking expedition we will transfer our photo onto a canvas with a wide white boarder and make a decoration to hang on our bedroom wall. We all have our own bedrooms and we will own the pictures. From this piece of artwork we will experience a sense of pride along with a great memory of another day with the Divas. Our Diva leader always tries to make our outing memorable.

After our hardy breakfast of eggs, beacon, toast with jelly, and grape juice, we are ready to hit the trail. When we were all gathered in a circle, our Diva leader explained that we would be having a forest ranger accompanying us today on our hiking expedition because of a reported sighting of Bigfoot in the area. She assured us there was no reason for alarm because Bigfoot would be more afraid of us then we would be of him.

After my dream, I'm glad a forest ranger, with a gun on his hip, is joining us. It brings comfort to my mind. The Bigfoot of my dream meant me no harm, however if there are communities of Bigfoot, like what was being discussed at the dinner table, we could run across a group of Bigfoot bad guys. Society has got people who are out of control, Bigfoot is a person, and a forest ranger has the ability to get him back in control.

Our Diva leader explained that Bigfoot is just a giant man, and that the Bible has writings of giant's so it's really not anything new, we just aren't accustomed to seeing these giants.

As we all load our backpacks onto our bodies Crystal said, "I do hope your dream doesn't come true, I have a tendency to get really scared easily, and I don't like that feeling."

"Don't worry Crystal, Bigfoot is only a very large man and no one has ever been hurt by a Bigfoot. I personally think Bigfoot is from the Stone Age and he is a Neanderthal or Cro-Magnon man that just did not evolve. After all, the world is 4 billion years old and if you drive outside of most cities there is miles and miles of land that no man has ever walked on. This world is very big and we are still finding tribes of people that have never been seen. My belief is that we develop according to what we are taught and our offspring inherit our memory cells. That's why we are so smart. If Bigfoot lives in remote areas and lives off the fat of the land, then his offspring would do the same. They would inherit Bigfoot's anti-social way and be very skilled at hunting and living on roots and making their homes in caves. Bigfoot is living much like an animal and this causes him to look different than modern man. Scientist can tell how old mankind is by the deep-sea cores from the ocean. This is how they can prove humans have always been human, only some have more education than others. Education is the key to passing our intelligence to our offspring. Our offspring will inherit our memory. That's why Bigfoot is the way he is, he's never been to school.

I believe Bigfoot survived the ice age because he is use to living high in the mountains where it's cold, and he knows how to hunt for food to stay alive. I believe we have ice age periods in different times because of volcano's erupting and ash filling the air, and the sun can't get through for plants to grow. Mount St. Helen is a good example of where Bigfoot lives. You see we are talking about fire and ice. Bigfoot can warm his toe over the volcano to stay warm while the rest of us freeze. During my parent's lifetime, Mount St. Helen erupted and Bigfoot's offspring were scattered throughout the United States. Since Mount St. Helen's eruption, there have been sightings all over the United State's. Bigfoot lost his main home because the ash killed everything that didn't leave.

Everyone agrees in the books I've read about Bigfoot, that he lives high in mountain areas. Most believe they live in south-facing caves to avoid the cold wind. By being high on a mountain they could avoid floods and could see anything coming that would be a threat to their safety. The cave would provide a climate control environment. Inside these caves is a carved out pool to collect rainwater. Large boulders that are round and can be rolled to cover the entrance for security at night. Also, the boulder is warmed by the sun and provides warmth in the cave. Can you image that Bigfoot is using solar technology before we even heard of it. Flint tools have been found in caves where Bigfoot has been living, according to those who found the flint tools. That means he can cook his food or warm his house in the winter. The flint tools also are used to cut meat and dig for roots. Only man can have such intelligence, so this proves Bigfoot is a man not an animal.

Many question the existence of Bigfoot because no bones have been found. The reason no bones of the dead have ever been found is because Bigfoot bury their dead in caves where different chemical properties destroy any bones that where placed in them. Some people think Bigfoot crushes the bones of their dead to avoid anyone or anything finding them. Who's to say Bigfoot is not intelligent enough to know that leaving any remains behind would lead to a full-scale search for him. After all, no one has caught Bigfoot, but many have seen him.

High up in many mountain caves, rocks have been placed in circles with a flat rock on top suggesting Bigfoot cooks on these stoves. Flint rock also has been found near these circles of rock, which Bigfoot uses to start a fire with. These findings and sightings of Bigfoot, has sparked renewed interest in the elusive Bigfoot, and everyone is sharing their information.

Another odd finding is all the quartz crystal rocks found in the caves. Could it be that Bigfoot found them pleasing to look at or do they also serve a purpose. Maybe the moon reflected quartz crystal light in the cave or could the quartz crystal be what Bigfoot considered art. We only know that a lot of people have seen him and he is very elusive and the evidence of his existence and quartz crystal cannot be denied.

I have no idea how long Bigfoot has been around but I do know that Africa is the cradle of humanity. This is where the hand-axe tool that only human beings posses have been found. Also the ability to have a language is only found in human beings. For thirty thousand years humans have been painting pictures on cave walls and writing their language by carving into the cave wall what they felt was important. Scientist all agree that mankind has always communicated in a high level of intelligence," Jan the Diva leader said.

This is so odd that Jan would have such a conversation that fits perfect with my dream. Could I subconsciously have heard all these things, and not be aware of it sometime in the past?

As I check my backpack, thoughts fill my mind about the dream I had. I pack a candy bar to leave at the top of Tiger Mountain for Bigfoot. I know his keen sense of smell will lead him right to it. I would like to see his face when he bites into it. Pure pleasure I'm sure.

We walked for near an hour when we came upon a clearing. There were huge rocks all over the place, and the Diva leader, suggested we take a break and find a rock to set on that suits us. Crystal found a rock big enough for both of us to sit on. We opened a bottle of water and took a load off our feet. Crystal pulled out a pocketknife, and began carving into the rock, "Chelsea and Crystal were here." Someday I will revisit this rock to see if the carving holds up to the elements. A small lizard scurries around our feet. We must be sitting on it's rock, it just keeps going back and forth and turns it's head occasionally to look us in the eye. It has no fear of us. I pulled out my camera to take a picture of the little guy. He cocked his head as if he was posing for the picture.

Jan pointed to another clearing around 100 yards away, and there was the group of people climbing a hill. They had a megaphone and told us they are looking for Bigfoot and asked us to wave our arms if we have seen him. They got no response and began moving towards the top of Tiger Mountain.

We heard voices coming down the trail, Crystal looked at me and said, "Do you hear what I hear?" I looked at her and shook my head as if to say yes. Along with the voices was the sound of branches breaking. It sounds like a lot of people. Maybe they are also in search of Bigfoot. He has caused quite a commotion around these parts. They are getting closer and closer and now the forest ranger and Jan are walking in the direction of the voices. A covey of quail fly straight up and Jan gave a little squeal when they flew all around her head, than they were off to the open air and out of sight. We could hear the forest ranger talking to someone and Jan was walking back towards us. She waved us into a group and said, "We have a group of Guy Troups that have been camping on the top of Tiger Mountain and they will be passing through. I invited them to take a break with us if they want. Girls, please be on your best behavior."

As they filled into the open area each grabbed a rock to

sit on. The backpacks they were carrying were crammed full. They looked very heavy. Two mules also carrying supplies were right behind the Guy Troups. I immediately got up to pet the little mules, and shared a raw carrot that I was chewing on with them. A very friendly Guy Troup approached me and said, "The brown one's name is Buck and the gray one's name is Betsy. They seem to like you." This guy was looking me over and I broke the uncomfortable feeling with, "Animals always like to be fed, even if they are not hungry. Looks like they are a big help with this load on their backs. My name is Chelsea, glad to meet you." The boy held out his hand and said, "My name is Bruce and it's my pleasure. The mules are a great help. They carry our tents and canned food. We were up on top of this hill for three days. We had a great time. The path we take is longer because of the mules needing flat land to walk on, but that's okay because the load is too much for us to carry."

Jan came to give the mules a scratch behind the ear, and they loved it. Jan didn't say anything to us but looked us both in the eye, smiled and left. Bruce reached down into one of the bags the mules were carrying and pulled out a piece of bubble gum. He held it out on his hand and made a jester that it was for me. I reached for it and Bruce closed his hand immediately. I jumped for he startled me. He grabbed my hand and put the gum in it. We both began to laugh. I popped the gum in my mouth and blew a huge bubble and Bruce popped it with his finger.

"You know this mountain is a dead zone for cell phones. However you can pick up two radio stations. I heard there has been a Bigfoot sighting at the bottom of this mountain. The radio said, that a group of Bigfoot, enthusiast, are searching these mountains as we speak. What do you know about this?" said Bruce.

"Yes you are right. Bigfoot was spotted by a boy named Scottie, and people from all over are in search of Bigfoot. Even a boy named Kale from Japan is here with his family to join in the search. Kale, also seen a red haired Bigfoot, in Japan, some time back. The one Kale and the one Scottie seen are both red haired. Most think these are young Bigfoot's because they came so close to the boys, also a print was found that indicated this Bigfoot is young. Most adult Bigfoot's are seen at a great distance, they are very elusive," I said.

"We found a large pile of bones near where we were camping and thought it odd that they were pilled up like they were. One of the guys stumbled upon them when he was looking for firewood. Our Troup leader marked the spot with a pole and a red tee shirt tied to the top. He wants the authorities to check it out when we get back to town. They looked like deer and wild boar bones. I picked up this tusk from the pile of bones and it must be five inches long. How far up are you girls going Chelsea?" said Bruce.

"We will take two more hours to reach our destination. We are going where the bluebells are, you know the flowers. The blue butterflies, are suppose to be there, and we are going to find them. We plan to photograph the butterflies and turn them into pictures to hang on the wall of our bedrooms, you know, artwork," I said.

"Yes we passed through the very field you are talking about and there are plenty of beautiful butterflies for you to enjoy. The butterflies, were landing all over us, it was really neat. You will enjoy your day. We spent an hour there ourselves taking a break and eating lunch," said Bruce.

The Diva leader Jan is gathering all the girls together to continue the journey up Tiger Mountain when Bruce handed me the wild boar tusk. "You may need this for protection," Bruce said. "Thank you Bruce, I feel safer already. I've got to go, glad you talked to me, I enjoyed it, bye bye," I said.

Going up hill makes for a slow walk. It will be at least two more hours before we make it to the butterfly field. I'm excited about taking pictures of the blue butterflies and turning them into a picture pasted on a canvas with a frame. It will be my masterpiece.

We hear a rustling in the brush just to the left side of the

Diva Girls and I begin to rub the wild boar tusk that Bruce gave me. Whatever that thing is in the bushes, it better look out for me, I'm armed with a deadly weapon. I do feel safer with this tusk in my hand and I won't hesitate to use it. It sounds like it is very big. Could it be Bigfoot? It's as if this thing is taking the same path that the Diva Girls are taking only ten feet to the left of us. Could it be stalking us? Why isn't it afraid of us? Most wild creatures want to get away from humans, not follow along beside them. Everyone is aware of this creature and there is chatter that maybe it is Bigfoot. I can feel the fear in the air. Some of the girls were saying it could be a pack of wild dogs, it sounds like more than one critter.

The forest ranger is walking all the way to the front of the line telling the girls to stay close to one another and be as quite as possible, no talking. I don't know if he is saying this to keep us from scaring each other, or if it is better indeed If we are quite. The girls have taken down the chatter to a whisper, and are holding hands. This is making us feel safer.

The forest ranger has now made it to the front of the line and is talking to Jan. They have their heads together like they are putting a plan together as to what they will do if a situation occurs. The forest ranger draws his gun out of its holster and is holding it close to his leg so the girls won't notice it. My dad hunts a lot so I'm use to seeing guns and it was the first thing I noticed on the forest ranger, that and his oversized hat. He must feel we are in harms way or he wouldn't have drawn his weapon. He gave Jan a smaller gun he was carrying under his vest. She looked to be uncomfortable with the gun, as the forest ranger gave her instructions on how to use it. He began to descend to the back of the line all the time looking to the left, trying to get a glimpse of the critter making all that noise.

We have a couple of girls who are sobbing in a quite under their breath sort of way. My heart goes out to them, fear is a terrible feeling and if you are in tears, you have lost control of your fear and it owns you.

Whatever this thing is, it is getting closer and closer, I can feel its presence. The rustling of the bushes is so close now we can see the brush moving. Everyone squatted down with the hand movement of our Diva leader Jan. The only person still on their feet is the forest ranger. The critters are now moving full speed right towards the center of the Diva Girls. The forest ranger has his weapon pointed in the direction of the moving brush. He has both hands on the weapon to steady his hands for the perfect shot. The closer the critter came the louder the brushes rattled and we could feel the vibration of the ground with the pounding of the feet. Suddenly a Buck Deer leaped over the girls just in front of me and two Doe Deer followed behind him. I never knew a deer could jump so high. The girls screamed to the top of their lungs and grabbed their heads as if to protect themselves from their fears. The forest ranger immediately went to comfort the girls who were crying and shaking all over. He showed these girls the trail that crossed right over the trail we were taking and told the girls that deer are creatures of habit and were just following the trail, and that everything is going to be okay.

It was as if a load was taken off my shoulders when I saw the deer's. I relaxed my hands that were holding the wild boar tusk much like the forest ranger relaxed his hand that held his gun after realizing it was only deer. Crystal looked at me with the tusk in my hand and wiped her forehead with a jester that indicated, that was a close one.

Jan came down the trail to comfort the girls who were so upset. She offered to take all of us back to camp if we all wanted to return. Everyone wanted to continue up the trail to our destination. We just needed to gather ourselves up.

Jan explained to all of us that deer are protected this time of year and therefore they are not afraid of humans. Somehow they know they are safe in the summer.

The mood is much lighter now that we know it was not Bigfoot stalking us. It is still in the back of every Diva Girl's mind that we could have an encounter with Bigfoot before the day is over, however, we are on a mission and no one wants to turn back and head for camp until our mission is complete.

The giggles are back as we all make fun of how we overacted to a situation with some harmless deer. They were quite beautiful with their white bellies flashing before our faces as they leaped over our heads. The imagination can take you places that are as real as if they are happening. I was scared out of my head and ready to stab the bogyman with my five-inch tusk. It was crazy. I'm laughing at myself now, but I truly was a lose cannon just a minute earlier.

This part of the trail is almost straight up hill. My legs are feeling every step as I grab a vine to help pull myself up and take some of the strain off my legs. The two girls following behind me are having trouble as well. One and all are feeling the burn in the calf of our legs. As I pull myself up with the vine in hand, my foot slips and my face went right into the dirt. Crystal burst out laughing as I spit dirt out of my mouth. Crystal pulled out a washcloth from her backpack and wiped my face. That was so nice. If I had stayed on the path this would never have happened. I wanted a challenge, it looked like fun, but a lesson has been learned about getting off the beaten path. When I got on level land it was time to get the water bottle out of my backpack and rinse my mouth out. I understand that dirt has a lot of minerals in it, but I would rather get my minerals through vegetables that pull minerals out of the dirt. They taste a lot better.

We have one more hour and we should arrive at our destination. I'm glad we are taking a little break. I used a lot of energy getting up that hill. In my backpack is a honey and oat bar and it should get everything back in order for me. I've worked up quite an appetite. Taste great.

The sun is creeping up this mountain and warming things up. The bluebell flowers should be reaching for the sun right about now and the butterflies will be feeding on their nectar. I can't wait to see them.

Jan and the forest ranger are pointing to a place on Tiger

Mountain that is in the opposite direction of the hill we are on. Some of the girls are joining them to see what it is that has captured their attention. As I joined them I caught a glimpse of a red creature darting in and out of the trees. It would not stay still long enough for us to get a good look at it. We could only get a glimmer, a brief flash of red. The creature seemed to move in a smooth, effortless way. The forest ranger got out his binoculars hoping to get a clear look so he could identify this creature. Then the forest ranger handed Jan the binoculars and said, "It's him, Bigfoot." Jan took the binoculars and began searching for Bigfoot. In the meantime, the forest ranger contacted his base with his two-way radio. He began with, "We have a sighting of Bigfoot two degrees south and five degrees west of the peak on Blue Cherry Pass. He is headed in the opposite direction of the Diva Girls Blue Butterfly destination. We will continue on our path to Wild Berry." The response was, "Copy that."

Jan was looking high and low with the binoculars but never got a glimmer of Bigfoot. She only seen what we seen, an unclear look at a reddish looking creature moving in and out of the trees. Some of the girls were taking pictures but it was so far away I doubt any of them will show much. I just keep clicking my camera hoping one of the shots will be a good one.

Everyone is so excited at the possibility of an actual Bigfoot sighting. Crystal said, "Girls we have made history today. When we get back down this mountain we will be added to the list of many who have seen Bigfoot. The evidence is patchy and incomplete through our eyes but the forest ranger got a clear look with his binoculars to give what we just seen as hard evidence. Earlier today myself, and Chelsea listened to a young boy tell a story of a sighting of Bigfoot in Japan. His Bigfoot had red hair just like the one we seen today.

The boy from Japan, named Kale, believes Bigfoot becomes more active when earthquakes and volcano's erupt. We have been having more and more active earthquakes in Oklahoma recently. Some are causing a lot of damage.

Kale talked a lot about a volcano called Krakatoa. He talked about how in 400 A.D. Kradatoa first erupted and it was a world-changing event with an enormous effect on the climate. Darkness filled the air because the dust shadowed the sun for eighteen months. The sun was only seen for about four hours a day.

He talked about how the noise was fearful and the thundering sky shook as the volcano spit fire into the air and when the fire fell it was like glitter on the ground. The white smoke is hot water vapor with a smell of sulfur. If the smoke from a volcano is white it is safe, but if it turns gray it is fixing to be dangerous. Krakatoa was blown all the way down to sea level, to nothing but burning ash.

Right here where we are standing, on Tiger Mountain, is the result of an earthquake. Plates deep in the earth are crashing into each other resulting in the earth above it, making mountains. All Bigfoot's, live in mountains, and volcano's according to their history. I learned this just the other day when Kale talked to a group of people who are right now, this very moment, looking for Bigfoot. All those experts are looking for Bigfoot, and a group of Diva Girls, are the ones to find him. Go figure."

Our short break is now over and its time to continue our journey to the bluebell fields. The trail is wider now and the trees are more spread out. We can now walk beside each other instead of in a column, single file. Crystal found this to be an opportunity to get to know me better. She started asking questions about my life.

"Tell me a little about yourself Chelsea Songbird," Crystal said.

"Let me start with I live in Tahlequah Oklahoma with my parents and sister Cloie. My father is an orphan and has no family but us. My grandparents on my mother's side of the family both died in a car accident last year. I was very close to my grandmother and it was devastating to lose her. She was the rock for our family's morals. Her motto was if you can live by the Word, The Bible, you will have a wonderful life. It has the answer for every moral question you have. If you drift very far from the teachings of the Bible you will have great sadness in your life.

At my grandparents funeral I was happy to know they were going to heaven but sad that I would never be able to talk to them again. They were the best people I've known in my life. I'm lucky to have had them in my life and thank God for them every day even though they are gone. I received a solid foundation of what is good in life and live my life based on that foundation. So far life is grand for me," I said.

"You are lucky to have guidance, and be so close to your family. My family is all messed up. My dad did a lot of drugs when he was young and bragged about it all the time. He talked about all the fun he had doing them and made it out to be a glamorous life. He seems to be a very miserable person to me. He based his life on doing all kinds of bad things and his greatest accomplishment was being able to stay out of prison for all the bad things he had done in his life. He was lucky to not get caught. My mom is not like him, she is a good person, if not for her, dad would be in prison today. She demanded he straighten up his life. My brother, however, idolized his dad and hung onto every story he told about his wild days, and became what dad bragged about being. My brother has been in prison for two years now. He thought drugs were cool because our dad talked about them all the time, and he became a drug addict. In order to get money for his drugs he became a seller of drugs. One day, he tried to sell drugs to a DEA agent. Big mistake! Now he will be spending a total of ten years of his life in prison. What a waste.

My mother divorced my dad and now I see him twice a month on weekends. I'm ten years younger than my brother and seeing what happened to him let me know how un-cool drugs are. My dad still refuses to acknowledge that his son, my brother, hung on every word he said and wanted to be just like him. My mother realized what happened to her son, only after it was to late. She is going overboard with me, she wants to be a shinning example for me, and it is paying off because I'm a good kid. I live in Chicago and my mother pays for me to go all over the United States in the Diva Girls outings. My mom was real easy with my brother, but she is doing everything in her power to point me in the right direction. Your parents do have a hand in how you turn out in life. It is the parent's responsibility to give their children guidance. Parents teach children how to act at a very early age and it stays with them their entire life. My mom taught me this and when I have children I will be very mindful of my actions around my children.

I'm also a very good student, straight A's. I'm always excited to go to school in the mornings. I've done summer school three years in a row and I take computer classes. Every summer I learn some really neat stuff. My mom encourages me to get as much knowledge about running computers as possible. Knowledge is power and knowledge pays real good wages in the workforce. You know when we grow up we will be joining the workforce and it would be nice to pick where we go to work.

I visit my brother in prison once a month. He has eight more years to go. Every time I visit him, he tells me how he wishes he could turn back the hand of time so he could make better choices. He tells me how he would never have touched a drug. He claims he was a prisoner to drugs even before he became incarcerated in prison. He just shakes his head and tells me how he misses his freedom. We always put money on the books for him so he can get a candy bar occasionally. Eight more years is a long time from now. You know I'll be 22 years old when he gets out," Crystal said.

"I'm sorry you have to go through such a heartache. Life is so fragile. We always want the best for the people we love, but we just can't control everything life throws at us. The people we love sometimes make bad choices," I said.

"This is why my mother is pointing me in the right direction every chance she can. She feels enormous guilt for what has happened to my brother's life. My mother educates me on ways to enjoy life drug free. She encourages exercise and any kind of sports. When the body is active, endorphin release, which are a group of hormones with tranquilizing and pain-killing capabilities that are secreted by the brain. She is so spot-on about being active. Another thing she does is to educate me on the importance of being together at the dinner table because this is where you learn manners. Back when dad was at home we just grabbed a plate and watched TV while we ate. That's history. Mother believes that by eating at the table I will learn how to interact while eating. This will prepare me for when I get a job and have to interact with my co-workers. Also she is able to teach me about portion control and the importance of a balanced meal. I have learned one very important thing, if the body doesn't get what it needs in nutrition it eventually breaks down.

What I personally like about all the changes my mother has made since she divorced my dad, is the time she now spends with me. If she had spent this much time with my brother, I believe he would be with us today instead of in prison. He desperately needed her guidance.

My mother has me pointed in the right direction and I know my life will be a good one until the end of my time on earth. The most impressive thing she told me is, everyone is born with a certain level of intelligence. We can tap into that intelligence with education. Our happiness and moods we have some control over with our diet. Drink eight glasses of water a day, eat broccoli and brussels sprouts at least four times a week. Strawberries and blueberries you can eat every day if you want but at least four times a week. Avoid sugar, white flour, soft drinks, and caffeine and other stimulants. What she tries to get through my head is that these things will keep me healthy and that will keep me in a good mood. I love her for showing me how to be happy," Crystal said.

"You know Crystal, my mom and dad think a lot like your mother. They press the importance of diet to keep healthy and happy. I also love them for teaching me how to make my life good. What my parents press on me most is the importance of family. They believe that if you demand the most out of every member of the family, than the family will be well adjusted and fit in with society. It takes a lot of work but it's worth it in the long run. What you are telling me about your family being all messed up is what my family tries to avoid. It would kill my soul if my sister, Cloie, went to prison for ten years. I feel so bad for you, and your mother and brother. It's a pain I hope I never have to experience. I wish I could do something to ease your pain," I said.

"You can Chelsea, make a beautiful family and protect that family from any bad influence. You will be married and raising children before you know it. Keep your family together and make your husband do right by the family. Children look up to the dad and will mirror him, good or bad. Promise me you will do this and my pain will be eased," Crystal said.

"I promise," I said.

"I've got a great idea Chelsea Songbird, let's take turns giving advice that will bring us happiness on this long road of life. I'll go first," Crystal said.

"Be humane to your pets, their not like critters you hunt for the dinner table," Crystal said.

"Be good natured," I said.

"Be gentle," Crystal said.

"Be loveable," I said.

"Always be honest," Crystal said.

"Try to be humble," I said.

"Be gracious," Crystal said.

"Always be fair," I said.

"Try to be supportive of others needs," Crystal said.

"Be sweet," I said.

"Protect your freedoms," Crystal said.

"Be responsive to changes," I said.

"Show ability to be exuberate," Crystal said.

"Be significant in someone's life," I said.

"Be enthusiastic about your life," Crystal said.

"Stay clean," I said

"Bring joy to others life," Crystal said.

"Encourage others to be kind," I said.

"Groom your hair daily, it is your crown," Crystal said.

"Discover your purpose in life," I said.

"Be proud of your accomplishments," Crystal said.

"Finish what you start," I said.

"Secure your future," Crystal said.

"Be independent," I said.

"Understand yourself," Crystal said.

"Be hopeful," I said.

"Enough already, I thought you would run out of things to say, but you are really good at this game. Looks like we will find the good life, without any problem. We sound like true Diva Girls. These are the things they stand for.

Let's get back to Bigfoot. Chelsea, what would you do if you came face to face with Bigfoot? Would you scream, turn and run, or try to talk to him," Crystal said.

"That's a good question Crystal. No one knows exactly what action they would take, that would be like predicting the future. However I have given this situation some thought. First thing I would do is turn on my camera and try to capture the audio part of the event, than I would try to raise the camera and capture some video of Bigfoot, that is if I'm not frozen in place with fear. I don't know if you noticed earlier, that when we seen that red dot on the other hill, that everyone thought was a Bigfoot, my camera was rolling. When we get back to town I'm taking this film to that group of people who are searching for him. I know they will be able to do things with this piece of film that I never could. They have the experts that would be able to blow the image up to a larger size that would be clear enough that we could determine just what we all seen. The forest ranger seems to think it was Bigfoot, after all he had binoculars that enlarge the image, and he thought it was a man shaped image that he was looking at. I'm certain with my documented image of Bigfoot, we will all become part of history, in the Bigfoot legion. You see Crystal, it's not a question of what would I do if I seen Bigfoot, it's a statement of what I did do, when I saw Bigfoot," I said.

"Your right Chelsea, you have proven his existence on video already. You are going to be famous. That is famous around Bigfoot followers, which are all over the world. When we get back to camp I want your autograph. I will keep it forever," Crystal said.

I just rolled my eyes and picked up the pace going up the hill. I reached in my pocket and pulled out a pack of gum. I put one in my mouth and handed the other over my shoulder to Crystal. Chewing gum will help take my mind off this almost straight up hill that is zapping all my energy.

Crystal popped the gum in her mouth and started talking again. This girl can talk non-stop. Here I'm just trying to catch my breath and Crystal is running her mouth again.

"I wonder if Bigfoot has a family with marriage and kids and the whole civilized thing, only in Bigfoot law. If so, I wonder if they ever get divorced and the children suffer like the so-called civilized human beings do. You know the marriage vows say 'until death do you part,' but half of most marriages end up in divorce and the children suffer for what the parents did. Do people get married just because they like the way someone looks, and later they realize they don't like the personality of the person they married? Do they go into the marriage with the idea that if it doesn't work they can always get a divorce? Do they even think about what they are doing to their children? All I know is that the kids who come from a divorced family have a lot of emotional baggage that is difficult to deal with. It just doesn't seem fair for them to have to deal with all the sadness associated with their parent's problems. I hope there is no divorce in the Bigfoot world." Crystal said.

We made it up this steep hill and I'm catching my breath. It's as if talking gives Crystal extra energy, just the opposite for myself. I can hardly catch my breath much less talk non-stop while climbing up this hill.

"My guess is that Bigfoot doesn't believe in divorce. Bigfoot is closer to nature in my opinion, and the family unit needs to take care of one another in the more primitive world. After all, Bigfoot must protect his family from all the humans that are searching for them. If indeed we did find him, it would change the way he and his family lived forever. They would be on public display and dissected like a wild animal." I said.

I image that Bigfoot is more concerned with providing food, shelter, and safety for his family. When you are concerned with your family's welfare, you are less concerned with your own needs. I think that modern day humans are caught up in the, 'I factor'. They are consumed with their needs, and put their wants above their children's needs. They always want things their way and will destroy the family unit if need be to get their way. In the end the whole family suffers.

This great country has been in many wars to protect our freedoms, yet when most families get divorced it's because one of the two who are married want to take away all the freedom of the other. An example would be if the husband loved going fishing with his male friends before he got married, and after he got married, the wife wanted this to end. She would forbid her husband to have fun fishing with his friends. He immediately feels his freedom is being taken away and the war is on.

The whole fishing thing will take care of itself with time if the wife is just patient. As the husband matures, he spends less and less time with his friends and more and more time with his family. He let's go of his hobby when the time is right for him, this way there is no resentment. He is not being told to stop going fishing, he just grew out of the whole thing, and he starts taking his family fishing with him for company. I'm just using fishing as an example, it could be golf or bowling or any sport that took him away from the family.

My point is, just because you marry someone, you don't

own the life given to that person, by the parents. When you start taking away their freedom you start destroying the marriage. If the husband, or wife, is having more fun at home, than out fishing with their buddies, she or he will be at home more often. Home needs to be a place where the husband and wife want to be, not a place where they want to get away from. I believe it takes a lot of work to make home a good place to live, however, it's worth the hard work. The whole family benefits when the home is a fun place to be.

It is my belief that all Bigfoot's don't even know what a divorce is. They are to busy taking care of each other to even think about kicking a member of the family out. Instead of calling Bigfoot primitive and unsophisticated, we could learn a thing or two from them. With all our smarts we have yet to catch one of them," I said.

Crystal became very quiet, I guess she is trying to digest the thought that Bigfoot could possible have it together better than this educated society we are living in. The kids in my school who come from broken families get very sad when they talk about their parents getting divorced. It is as if they think it is partly their fault, when in reality they have nothing to do with the reason their parents got a divorce.

I have one friend whose parents have joint custody and this works great for her. She spends two weeks with her dad, and than two weeks with her mom. No one has to pay child support this way, and the parents have no financial pressure each month. Also, my friend feels a real bond takes place when she is around either parent for two straight weeks. All the resentment of having to pay child support goes out the window and the parents want to make her happy. She has her own room at each of their houses and never needs to pack a bag. She has clothes in the closet and socks in the drawers when she gets there. She does her own laundry and takes turns doing the dishes and cleaning the houses. She said her parents get along better apart than they do together. They even invite each other over for dinner occasionally. She thinks when they grow up they might even get married again to each other. Wouldn't that be a great thing for her?

Family is one of the most precious gifts anyone can ever receive and it must be protected beyond all other needs in life. My mother taught me this at a very early age. We would discuss the word, 'relationships,' on a regular basis. It is the one thing she said would bring us happiness in life. Not money, not cars, and not things we think are of material value, but being able to get along with other human beings, having relationships, good relationships. Mother would say we need to be open to others needs to be heard. We have to give our time to listen to others even if we disagree with what they have to say. They must be allowed to express their thoughts. The more a person is allowed to talk the more there is a chance you will find something you have in common with them. When you find this thing you bond behind it. If you can find what that person thinks is their purpose in life, you will begin to know them to their core.

I have a friend who is the eternal pessimist. She always looks at the dark side of things, where I'm just the opposite, the bright side of things appeal to me, the eternal optimist. My friend is so pessimist that she drives herself into a depression occasionally. She suffers terrible from the condition. She learned this behavior from her mother. Her mother always thought the worst of any possible outcome. Growing up my friend thought this is what you do, look for the worst in every situation. I try to tell my friend that what she thinks effects how she feels. It can make her sad, angry, even embarrassed if she lets bad thoughts rule her mind.

One day in the cafeteria, my friend was really hungry and loaded her tray with food. One of the older kids said, 'you are eating like a pig, oink, oink.' My friend was so embarrassed she did not eat a bite of her food for the first ten minutes of lunch. Finally I said to her, 'Do not let that jerk ruin your lunch today with his rude remarks. The problem is, he just said that because he has a weight problem. He's jealous because you can eat all this food and never gain an ounce.' After putting my spin on the situation, she picked up her fork and cleaned her plate. She told me that I was good for her. I took away the thoughts that she was being a pig, and made her realize her thoughts were not true that the boy put in her head.

The relationship we have built by listening to each other's fears has created a strong bond that is very beneficial. I get a feeling of being able to encourage my friend to look at things in a different light, a bright light instead of a light that's about to go out, and it makes me feel good to take away some of her darkness.

Joining the Diva Girls group opened my eyes to the fact that people must let go of past hurts, pains, and failures in order to move forward in life. What one conceives in life is directly connected to how they believe. We must believe that life can be good for us, and it will be great, this I learned from Jan, our Diva leader.

I share the good things I learn in life with my friends to help make their life better. Jan taught me that helping others with my knowledge, on life's road to happiness, makes me a better person. These are gifts to others to open their eyes to a better life. They can take them or leave them. It is their choice.

The biggest gift I've ever given to a friend is the knowledge of the favor of God. You must become favor-minded in order to receive favor from God. If God is pleased with your actions, you may ask Him for His favor, and receive it. God's favor can turn any situation around, through faith. We are all made in the image of God and knowing this gives us a positive self-image that we carry through life's challenges.

If the image of yourself is what God says you are, than you should be on cloud nine all the time. You have the ability to rise above your raising if you come from an abusive family environment. Or if someone says hurtful words about the way you look or about the clothes you ware, you can let it roll off you like water on a ducks back. God is your armor and will protect you from all evil. Your deep-down feeling of your self-worth is 'you matter in life.' This is God's gift, and if you accept it you will always like yourself. If you can do this you give yourself the gift of happiness for a lifetime. So feel good about yourself, God loves you always.

When we love ourselves like God loves us, unconditionally, it doesn't matter if our nose is to big for our face, or if we are to skinny or overweight. We are created by God the way we are and He loves what he created. Who are you to say what God created is not perfect for His plan?

God empowers you to be the person he created, you must accept the gifts he gives you, and do what He commands. Everyone has value that God gave them, it is inside our souls and we must search our hearts and bring it out for all to see. God created us so we must have good deeds inside our soul. If we read the Bible it will show you how to tap into your good side, this is Gods gift to you, His Word.

With Gods armor on you can guard yourself from Satan, the Devil. "When an evil spirit comes out of a man, it goes through arid places seeking rest and does not find it. Than it says, 'I will return to the house I left.' When it arrives, it finds the house unoccupied, swept clean and put in order. Then it goes and takes with it seven other spirits more wicked than itself, and they go in and live there. And the final condition of that man is worse than the first. That is how it will be with this wicked generation." Matthew 12:43-45.

The Devil is real. You must know this in order to protect yourself from Satan. If you let your guard down the Devil will try to come into your life and cause destruction of your soul.

My mother gives me the gift of knowledge to protect me from the Devil. She introduced me to the Bible and we study on a regular basis the meaning of God's Words. My mother wants me to be an angel in heaven when I leave this world. Her favorite passage in the Bible is, "You are in error because you do not know the Scriptures or the power of God. At the resurrection people will neither marry nor be given in marriage; they will be like the angels in heaven," Matthew 22:29-30.

My favorite passage in the Bible is, "Listen and understand. What goes into a man's mouth does not make him 'unclean,' but what comes out of his mouth, that is what makes him 'unclean.' But the things that come out of the mouth comes from the heart, and these make a man 'unclean.' For out of the heart comes evil thoughts, murder, adultery, sexual immorality, theft, false testimony, slander. These are what makes a man 'unclean'; but eating with unwashed hands does not make him 'unclean,'" Matthew 15:11,19,20.

The passage in the Bible that I protect myself with is, "Get behind me, Satan! You are a stumbling block to me; you do not have in mind the things of God, but the things of men," Matthew 16:23. The greatest gift you can give yourself is protection from the Evil One through God's Word.

The Bible is my favorite book to read. I recall a passage in Genesis 6:4, "There were giants in the earth in those days; and also after that, when the sons of God came in unto the daughters of men which were of old, men of renown." Is this where Bigfoot came from? Have there always been giants on earth? I plan to study the Bible when I get home to see if this passage is talking about Bigfoot.

Chapter 4

A Sighting

The park ranger radioed to the base camp the possible sighting of a Bigfoot. We could hear the cheers from the group listening to the radio and the excitement in the air was thick enough to cut it with a knife. In the background we could hear, 'Let's pack our gear, he won't escape our camera this time, be sure to get the net and let's take Bigfoot a candy bar.' This group is super excited to get a chance to see Bigfoot in the raw.

"We must get organized and bring plenty of gear, we may be in pursuit of Bigfoot for as many as four days. The area that the park ranger claims to have seen Bigfoot is straight up the side of a very rocky hill. It will take everything we have as a team to make it up that steep slope. Be sure to pack your hammers, pegs and plenty of rope. We don't want to have to come back down that hill because we need more rope. Jack, you are in charge of food, be sure to pack plenty of beef jerky. It will give us something to chew on when we don't have time to stop and cook a meal. There is a clear stream of water half way up the hill that runs non stop this time of the year, so pack water accordingly. The first six miles we will be able to ride our horses and the mules will be able to go several extra miles after that. The mules have better footing and are only carrying supplies. The last four miles we are on foot and if we have to go over the hill and down the other side to get a glimpse of Bigfoot, than we will have another twenty miles to search for him. The trees are thick and this will make our task more difficult to deal with," said Dr. Ben Holt.

"We will be entering territory where no human has ever walked. That's some pretty exciting stuff," said Dr James Nile.

"As a team we will all get recognition for whoever snaps a picture of Bigfoot. We know he is out there somewhere because of the eyewitness, Scottie. We also think this particular Bigfoot is a teenager. No adult Bigfoot would let anyone get that close to him.

After we reach the top of Tiger Mountain and start down the other side we need to stay close enough that we have a visual of the team members on both sides of you. We don't want anyone to lose their self in this boundless beauty of hills and forests. We may turn our minds from the myth of Bigfoot to the reality that Bigfoot is a man living true freedom, embracing a harmonious relationship with the natural world, paradise. We have not been raised in the wilds of nature, so I'm not sure we could survive, as Bigfoot does.

We have four mules and seven horses that are ready for us to mount and start our journey. We have thirteen team members so let's double up where we can with the light in weight, so not to stress the horses or mules. Kale and his dad can ride the mules that are not carrying a lot of supplies, the one's carrying blankets and pillows. Let's get started," said Professor Sprinkle.

Kale Taira, a Japanesse fourteen year old boy and his dad, choose the smallest mule to ride since together they only weigh 180 pounds. Kale is beside himself with shear joy at the thought of seeing a Bigfoot. Kale and his father were in search of Bigfoot in Oregon for a month when he heard about Oklahoma having a sighting, and with the idea that this Bigfoot could be a teenager, makes it that much more exciting for Kale.

In Japan, Kale claims to have seen a teenage Bigfoot in his town of Beppu. Kale claims that because we have been having a lot of earthquakes in Oklahoma recently, that has Bigfoot on the move. Kale says that when the earthquakes start in any area on earth, that Bigfoot is spotted in these areas. Could this be true?

Everyone is mounted on the horses and mules and they are starting the hunt for Bigfoot. There are no trails where Bigfoot was sighted so the hunting party is taking the paths of least resistance. The new trail they are making is anything but straight. It's swirling in every direction, missing trees, thick brush, and rocks as big as boulders. It's a good thing everyone has a compass to keep them going in the right direction.

The sun is shinning on the search party's back and a light sprinkle is freshening things up at the same time. A yellow, green and red rainbow is covering Tiger Mountain from one end to the other. This is one of God's truly beautiful gifts to mankind.

It's as if the vegetation is stretching toward the sky to drink up the light rain. The lush green becomes plump right before our eyes. It is nature at it's best, and the group is experiencing total harmony between humanity and nature.

This group is experiencing what Bigfoot lives in on a daily basis. I believe Bigfoot lives in harmony and peace without greed, or disease, they live with and in their natural surroundings, in communities, for protection from the wilds of nature.

The mystic status of Bigfoot being a savage killer of animals for survival is overstated. The fact is, Bigfoot is a concerned and thoughtful ecologists by preventing the over population of deer. They actually protect nature's potential vulnerability by thinning out the deer population. Nature in reality is a collection of destructive forces and Bigfoot is a fierce predator who provides meat for his family by hunting. The female Bigfoot collects berries and plants food near their cave, it's called farming, while the male Bigfoot hunts. I must admit that hunting would be much more fun than farming but also much more dangerous.

The romantic Noble Savage, Bigfoot, lacks the civil society that makes laws therefore he is free to live with nature that will nourish his spirit. Bigfoot has true appreciation of the death of an animal which nourishes his family daily, because he kills the animal, it's very different than ordering a hamburger from a fast food restaurant. You see we have been transformed from wild to domestic. We humans take the death of the animal for granted. All we think about is how good this greasy hamburger taste, not what took place to put it between two pieces of bread. We, and our natural environment, are integrally linked, yet we give no thought of the man who kills the cow for the hamburger we eat. We are totally disconnected. In this department, Bigfoot is one up on us.

This sweeping canvas of lush greenery has the entire search party feeling nature at it's very best the way Bigfoot feels every day. The beauty in the natural world is paradise and fills ones soul with natural joy. Everyone is feeling a kaleidoscopic of hypersensitive reactions to the paradise of therapeutic greenery, red berries, fresh washed air, and the brightly colored rainbow. It's as if the joy is pouring out of the pores of their skin emitting harmony and beauty in every direction and all are feeling the same thing.

It's funny how beauty calms the mind and how everyone shares the tranquility of a gleam hidden in an evergreen forest. The serene feeling, free from agitation the mind creates due to outside interference, nature brings joy. The only thing filling up the minds at this moment is the chirping of the birds and the footsteps of the animals gently touching the fallen leaves and twigs. The freshness of the air, and moistness on their faces, give a peaceful feeling. This moment is shared by all without words, free from disturbance of their normal daily activities.

The mule carrying the supplies, is the front leader of the search party. Professor Sprinkle felt this mule would be like a scout, and if anything dangerous lies ahead, this mule would stop in its tracks to let everyone know something is not right up ahead. After three hours of almost straight up climbing, the land began to level off. This was a great reprieve for the animals. They can all see level land is only temporary and so the group decided to take a break. The lead mule was drinking from a small spring feed pond and soon the others joined him. The search party removed the canvas covering the supplies and spread it on the ground like a blanket. Each lay down and stretch their legs, some not use to ridding rubbed their legs like they were already feeling the tightness horse-back ridding can cause if one doesn't ride often. A bottle of Absorbine Jr. provides rapid relief for the team's sore muscles, and its being passed around to those in need.

Everyone had a bite to eat and a drink of water. Staying hydrated is very important during the daylight hours. The team's energy level also is sustained with this small meal.

Kale was walking around and stretching his legs when he came upon some blackberry bushes and gave a holler out to the team to come have some desert with him. Everyone filled their bellies and picked extra to take for a snack latter.

Everyone takes part in repacking the mule, Lilly Bell, so the search for Bigfoot can begin for another three hours. The team wants to get as far up the hill as possible before nightfall. That way they can find a nice flat piece of land to throw their sleeping bags on, and get some rest.

The team is following single file with Lilly Bell leading the pack, when suddenly everyone came to a stop. Lilly Bell is sinking into a mud like pool of slime. She is struggling but is only sinking deeper in the slime. Professor Sprinkle radios back to the base camp. He needs advice on how to get Lilly Bell to safety.

Everyone has dismounted and are gathered on the banks of this mud hole. Professor Sprinkle threw a rope around Lilly Bell's neck but it is useless in this situation, she doesn't even budge when he tries to pull.

Professor Sprinkle finally gets a response to his hand radio. "This is base camp and we have a possible solution to your situation. We have your location and are sending a helicopter with a trampoline bed, and some rope. If you can maneuver the trampoline under the belly of the mule with the long pole and than take it over the back of the mule, you can tie ropes through the eyelets and onto the horses saddles and pull the mule out of the mud hole," Leon from base camp said.

Professor Sprinkle said, "That sounds like a great idea, can you send a pole with a hook on the end of it so I can tie the rope to the hook, this mud hole is around fifteen feet across." "Copy that," Leon said.

The helicopter arrived in 45 minutes and Lilly Bell is showing signs of stress. Her breathing is sounding labored and her ears are hanging down. Moisture is streaming from the corner of her eyes, as if she is crying.

The team hurries to guide the supplies being lowered by the helicopter to a flat piece of land. They unhook the net and wave to the helicopter good by. Professor Sprinkle immediately began to put the pole together while other team members spread out the trampoline matt to position it for the pole to be connected. Other team members position themselves to grab the trampoline matt once it is under the belly of Lilly Bell and on the other side of the mud hole.

The plan is perfect. The trampoline is in place, wrapped around Lilly Bell belly, and the team is attaching ropes to the horse's saddles and running the rope through the eyelets of the trampoline.

Leon radioed in a message, "We have a vet on board do you need us to lower him to look at that mule." Professor Sprinkle said, "Absolutely, this mule is in a lot of stress, I'm not sure she will make it, she is shaking all over."

The helicopter began to lower the vet and at the same time the horses began to pull Lilly Bell out of the green slime. Lilly Bell began to struggle like she is trying to help. In no time at all she is out of the slime and on her feet. A little wobbly, shaking all over, but standing. The vet immediately got into his bag, pulled out a very long needle and gave Lilly Bell a shot. He suggested we clean her up as best we can with the water and rags he brought with him, and suggested we make camp and start our journey in the morning. By than Lilly Bell will be as good as new. We all agreed and the vet motioned for the helicopter to drop the ladder once again. The vet climbed the ladder and the helicopter was out of sight in just a few minutes.

Lilly Bell was beginning to regain her composure as the team got the last of the green slime off her body. The shot the vet gave her is working. Her ears are back straight up and she took a couple of steps. Everyone started clapping with joy as Lilly Bell stumbled around and headed for some grass to eat. They knew she would be okay when she began to eat.

Kale with his curious nature stumbled across some dropping with what looked like plum seeds in it. Professor Sprinkle said, "This looks like bear droppings, they cannot digest plum seeds, and their droppings are a way for the seed to reproduce more plum trees. If we look around I'm sure we can find some wild plums."

Kale took the Professors advice and off he went, with his dad right behind him. The team began to unpack the supply. Lilly Bell is in great appreciation of her load being lightened. The sleeping bags are placed in a circle around where the fire will be burning. The team hoped to be closer to the top of Tiger Mountain, but Lilly Bell needs her rest. Professor Sprinkle began gathering dry wood to start a campfire. The others joined in and before to long, there is enough wood to keep the fire going all night long.

Ham and beans is on the menu for tonight with fresh made cornbread. There is nothing like cornbread made in a cast iron skillet with butter drizzled on top.

Suddenly out of the bushes Kale and his dad appeared with the bottom of their tee shirts holding lots of plums. Kale said, "Me and my dad are serving desert tonight. We have at least fifty plums here in our shirts." They poured them out onto one of the sleeping bags and grabbed a plate to join the others for supper.

Chapter 5

Blue Butterflies

Crystal pointed to the first blue butterfly any of us had seen. Its wing spread must have been at least three inches wide. It is the most beautiful thing I've ever seen.

Crystal said, "Look there is another and another." As we toped the hill on the flat part of Tiger Mountain, a meadow is filled with Bluebell Flowers and Blue Butterflies hovering above each of them. We all stood for a moment in ah of what lay before our eyes, just drinking it all in. The sunlight is splashing through the butterflies blue wings, brightening the blue color into a luminous, full of light, breath taking sight, prettier than any we have ever seen. This is what the trip is all about, blue butterflies, it is well worth the adventure of climbing Tiger Mountain to arrive at this destination. Words cannot do justice to this magnificent sight before my eyes.

As the Diva Girls gather on the first flat piece of ground that we have seen for hours, silence is in the air. That is except for the fluttering of the wings of hundreds of blue butterflies. Its as if everyone is in a trance.

Jan, the Diva leader broke the spell this beautiful act of nature has put upon each and everyone of us with, "Girls it is time to start taking pictures and videos of this magnificent sight. We need memories of this day to reflect on the rest of our lives. Today will always put a smile on our faces when we remember this glorious day. This is truly one of

God's accomplishments that I want to thank Him for. This day is marked by great beauty and splendor that my spirit is drinking up. At this moment I glorify God and thank Him for this magnificent and delightful day. In my heart I give Him thanks and I hope each of you do the same."

Everyone put their hands together and their eyes lifted to the heavens in silence to talk to God personally, and give Him thanks with their thoughts.

Crystal was the first to snap a picture. She is fixated on one particular butterfly that seems to be larger than the rest. Crystal is following this butterfly with full focus like she has formed a fixation and is unable to break this neurotic behavior. I hope this butterfly doesn't fly off the side of this hill for I believe Crystal will fall off the hill with this strong attachment and persisting behavior she is displaying. The butterfly seems to be enjoying all the attention and at times it has Crystal spinning in circles as it flies above her head. I think it likes her blue hat. It does kind of look like a giant bluebell flower.

Crystal is amusing, but it is time for me to find my perfect bluebell flower with the perfect blue butterfly drinking nectar. I want to capture the colorful wings spread as far apart as possible and the antenna straight up in the air.

These butterflies are insects that have a long protruding tongue that dips deep into the bluebell flower for a drink of nectar, which gives it the beautiful blue color. This is nature at it's finest.

As I slowly walk through the bluebell flowers and butterflies I feel wings brushing against my skin ever so lightly. I'm near the center of the field when I see two butterflies sharing a bluebell flower. This is the photo I'm looking for. As I bend down with my eye looking through the camera I begin to take shots rapidly as if I might miss the perfect shot. The eyes protruding on the top of the butterfly's head are dark in color, and they are looking into each others eyes like they are best friends, sharing a blue malt. The flower is full of sweet nectar, enough for two, and they are not leaving anytime soon. As I move to shoot from a different angle the butterflies spread their wings out to display all the beauty they posses. I take a shot from the top and as I look through the lens of the camera it's like I'm looking into two beautiful blue eyes, with gold speckles. After three snaps of the camera, both take off in flight together.

Now that my attention has been broken from two best friends sharing the blue malt through their straw like mouths, I get up from my knees to once again gaze across the beautiful fields of bluebells and butterflies. The beautiful sight takes my breath away. Before I begin shooting again I'm going to just drink in all this beauty without any distractions.

"Chelsea Songbird are you all right," said Jan. "Yes I'm fine, I just got caught up in the moment," I said.

I walked from one end of the field to the other taking shots of what I thought were magic moments for me, so I can always remember this day. I even get a shot of Crystal with a butterfly on her shoulder and her looking at it. I know she will appreciate it when I give her the picture.

It's time to set up our tents, before it gets dark. Jan found a nice flat piece of land under some trees where the bluebells, do not grow. We wouldn't want to disturb any of the butterflies.

Pitching a tent is a lot of work and the Divas work in pairs. Two in each tent and Crystal is sharing with me. First we put the pegs in the ground with a hammer, than attach the tent and assemble the poles, than get the tent in the air. The tent has windows with mesh to keep out the bugs. It's nice weather so I roll up the windows so the fresh air can fill the tent. We will be sleeping in sleeping bags so we will be plenty warm.

Now that everyone has the shelters in place, it is time to gather wood for our campfire. We need enough to last all night. Hopefully the fire will scare critters away. We find a dead tree around what would be a city block from our campsite. Jan has an axe to take apart the dead tree and each of us takes our turn on the end of the axe. Than we gather up the wood and head for camp. It took three trips to get all the wood.

The fire is going strong and now it's time to cook dinner. We each have a piece of lean stake that we roast over the fire on a stick. It is very tasty. Potato's are wrapped in foil and baked in the fire until soft. For desert all have roasted marshmallow.

On the hill where Bigfoot was spotted we see the campfire of the group in search of Bigfoot. The forest rangers are sending messages back and forth with flashlights. From what I hear the forest ranger and Jan talking about, everything seems to be okay with the search party but no sign of Bigfoot yet.

Now that everybody has their bellies full, it's time for sharing personal stories about each of our lives. We go in a clockwise direction and no subject is off limits unless it is in poor taste. Jan makes sure we don't get to far out in left field. She also gives advice if anyone requests a solution to a problem.

The first Diva to tell a personal story is Lisa. "My parents got a divorce three months ago and it has affected my ability to make good grades. I was a straight A student and now I'm lucky to make C's and D's. I even made a F on a English paper. I can't seem to remember what I just read. I've crawled into a shell and seldom even speak to anyone. I'm ashamed of the F I made on my English paper and I'm afraid if things don't get better I will fail English. I've lost all interest in life's pleasures such as sports and even TV. If my grades continue to get worse I will have to quit the Diva Girls, the only thing I still enjoy. If anyone has a suggestion to help me, I'm all ears," Lisa said.

"Lisa I'm sorry you are going through this bad time in your life. Divorce always causes pain for everyone involved. What's going on with you right now is that you are depressed. You are taking this personal, like it's your fault, and it is not your fault. Adults make their own choices in life and often times their children blame themselves, because they are just to young to understand adult problems. Lisa, every school has a counselor who can give you advice on how to deal with this very situation. Don't wait until it's to late, get in there right away. You don't want long-term depression to set in, and become part of your life. Right now you are feeling helpless, its up to you to walk into that counselors office and ask for help," Jan said.

"Thank you Jan, I will do just that on Monday," Lisa said.

Next to tell all is Trina.

"Thank you Lisa for sharing your story with us. I can relate to what you are going through only my parent's are still together but they fight all the time. They say awful things to each other and I believe they would be happier divorced than married. I have sad thoughts all the time because my mother is always crying because of the fighting. I'm always sick at my stomach and a lot of times I can't even eat. Just the thought of eating makes my stomach turn. I feel helpless just like you do Lisa. Why do I get sick to my stomach Jan?" Trina asked.

"Sometimes helplessness causes physical illness and the mind is causing this illness. You need to address this helplessness by talking about it like you are now, to your parents and to the school counselor if need be. You see the mind runs the body. If your thoughts are causing you to be sick because they are bad thoughts, than happy thoughts will make you feel good all over. Stop thinking sad thoughts that make you feel weak and helpless and start thinking happy thoughts and see if you feel better. You see Trina, when children see their parents sad because of all the fighting, it disturbs the child and long-term depression can set in. All this fighting between your parents could cause harm to you in a lasting way. You see you can remain highly depressed long after your parents have stopped fighting. You need to set down with your parents and have a long conversation with them about your feelings, you see thought and emotion affects the body, your parents need to know what their behavior is doing to you," Jan said.

I'm next in line and I think it's time for a more upbeat personal story. "I feel your pain Lisa and Trina. I feel it in the story you both told and in your voice as it became shaky. With time I know both of you will pull out of the depression you are feeling, and when you grow up and start your families, no way will you let this happen to them.

My parents taught me early in life that with optimism you can possible stop depression, by disputing your negative thoughts. My parents instilled in me the belief that there is a lot of good to life, more than meets the eye. You see my dad is an orphan and had been raised as an orphan in an orphanage. This caused him a great amount of pain because he had this longing to know his parents. By not knowing how to deal with this empty spot in his heart, he felt he wasted his youth by being a pessimists. He would wallow in the fact that he did not have a family life. When he tells the story it even makes me sad to this day.

Dad instilled in me that optimists recover from momentary helplessness immediately. It took dad half his life to figure this out and he wanted myself and my sister Cloie to be armed with optimists tools early in life. You see my family is very tightly knit and we share every bit of knowledge we acquire that can improve life. This is our gift to one another.

Dad tells us that if he hadn't experienced pessimist views at an early time in life he may not have been able to guard his family against the pain that comes with being a pessimist. This is why I know that Lisa and Trina will do everything in their power to secure the happiness of the family they will create in the future," I said

Now it's time for Crystal to share a personal story.

"Okay guys here we go. One day a pigeon landed next to our barn. It is white with red eyes and red legs. She truly is a beautiful bird. I opened the barn door and guided the pigeon into the barn by spreading my arms out and going left when the pigeon went left and right when the pigeon went right. Eventually she winded up in the barn and I closed the door behind us. I got a net and cornered the pigeon and netted her with ease. It's like she said, 'Okay I give up.' I than scoped her up out of the net and she began cooing. The sweetest song I've ever heard. I began talking to her and she cocked her head to the side and looked at me like she knew what I was saying to her. It was so cute.

I noticed that she had a leg band on and knew she was someone's bird. I contacted the police to see how to find the owner and they put me in contact with a lady who raises homing pigeon. I took the bird to her home and she checked out the number on the band against the numbers in her book and yes it belonged to her. She could tell I became very attached to this pigeon and asked if I wanted to keep it. A big smile came across my face and a big yes jumped out of my mouth. I told her the bird was a girl, and the reason I know this is because she laid an egg. The lady suggested that she give me a male bird and let them hatch off a clutch of off-springs and she would pick the best of the bunch for payment of the male bird. I told her, 'you have a deal.'

The male bird was also white and now I have a total of six white homing pigeons. My plans are to start a business by releasing these birds at weddings as the bride and groom leave the church. I'm making a box, with cardboard, that is shaped like a heart. The bride and groom open the box and the birds fly out and return to my house. Everyone thinks they are doves, a symbol of love, and it is a breathtaking experience for everyone who sees it. That's the plan anyway.

The young birds are just now learning to fly and I'm so excited. I hope their parents teach them how to get back home on their first release. I don't think anyone really knows how the pigeons find their way back home but some think it is some kind of magnetic field that only homing pigeons can see.

I think this is what I want to do all my life. I may learn how to make wedding cakes also, since I'm already going to be there. It would be extra money. The best thing about my future job is that everyone is always very happy on a wedding day. It will be nice to work with happy people,"

Crystal said.

Now it's time for Marie to tell a personal story.

"I don't have anything as dramatic or as exciting as the stories we've all heard so far, but it will help you to get to know me better, seeing how I'm new to the Diva Girls. I moved here to Oklahoma from Texas two months ago and my parents thought that by joining the Diva Girls I could meet some new friends. They are so spot-on with that. You all are the best.

I have two younger brothers, eight and eleven, and it's my responsibility to keep them out of trouble for two hours after school five days a week. That's a lot of responsibility. My parents both work and they pay me $20 a week to watch my brothers. We ride our bikes when the weather is nice and play board games inside the house when it's not nice outside. So far life is good for me and I thank God every day of my life for that," Marie said.

Now it's time for Jill to tell a personal story.

"I started tap dancing lessons six months ago and it's a blast. I never knew my feet could make so much noise. It's a lot of hard work but it is so worth it. When I go to a recital and dance as a soloist I feel like a movie star. Dancing is deep in my soul and I will always tap dance for the joy it brings me. My instructor tells me I have this thing called rhythm that makes my feet work. I don't even have to think about it, I just let loose and my feet respond effortlessly," Jill said.

Now it's time for Alice to share her personal experience with the group.

"Cooking is where it is at. I make up my own dishes and this brings out my creative juices. It's like I take these wonderful vegetables and meats and turn them into mouthwatering delights. I want all of you to know that I'm very good at cooking, and it brings a great amount of joy into my day. I would like to share with you my version of Goulash:

2 pounds of hamburger, fried and drained

1 pound of hot sausage, fried and drained
Put all in big pot and add
20 cut up tomato
All your favorite vegetables cooked
3 diced and fried onions
1 large package of elbow pasta cooked and drained
Velveta cheese to your taste
Salt and pepper to your taste

That's all there is to it. Very simple and you can add whatever vegetables you want to make it more healthy. I encourage each of you to take an interest in cooking. Your future family will love you all the more for it. Enjoy the process of your creations," said Alice.

Next to tell her story is Joanna.

"Hold on, for you are about to hear the strangest story that I have experienced in the past, present, or future of my life. Two years ago I went to spend the weekend with my grandparents who live in the country. When I spend the weekend with my grandparents my chore is to feed, water, and collect eggs from the chickens, which I thoroughly enjoy.

One mid-afternoon, on a balmy day, dark clouds began to fill the sky. Within a matter of minutes the whole sky was dark and occasionally lit up with lightening. I wanted to finish feeding the chickens before heading for the house, when I heard my grandmother holler, 'hurry Joanna, we need to get into the storm shelter.' My grandfather was opening the door to the shelter and my grandmother started to descend underground. My grandfather motioned for me to join them. About that time the earth shook with a loud clap of thunder and the sky lit up with an electrical charge like none I've ever seen. It shook me to the very core of my body. I dropped my feed bucket and began running to the cellar. Before I made it to the shelter, the sky once again lit up with electrical charges and I felt my body was on fire as I melted and fell to the earth.

The next thing I knew I woke up in the hospital. My

grandfather filled in the details for me as the nurse was applying ointment to my burned body. I was burned from head to toe, especially my feet. You see, when you get struck by lightening, it burns the outside of your body where you are moist. That's why my feet got the worst burns, the sweating inside my shoes made moisture. I have permanent damage to my little toe on my left foot. I think that is where the lightening was exiting my body.

'Joanna my darling, the reason why you are in the hospital is because you were hit by lightening while running to the storm shelter. I picked you up, got you under ground, and called 911 on my cell phone. The ambulance arrived in minutes and brought you here. You have been unconscious for twenty hours. Me and your grandmother and the rest of the family have been taking turn's sitting with you. They are in the cafeteria right now eating lunch. I just got done with the chores at the farm and I want you to know the chickens are okay. I would give you a hug but you are as red as a lobster. The doctors say you are going to be fine, you are just really burned on the outside of your body, like a bad sunburn,' my grandfather said.

I stayed in the hospital for another two days and a week later my entire body began to shed the dead skin from the burn. Even my scalp lost its skin. It wasn't easy getting the skin out of my hair.

After my body healed it was time to heal my mind. I was afraid to be outside. Just walking in the grass with the open sky above without even a dark cloud in the sky brought fear into my heart. I began reading the Bible, looking for the answer. You see my family believes all the answers to their problems are in the Bible. Everyone must find their own answer to their unique problem.

As I read the Bible, I found the words 'fear not' 365 times in the Bible. Oddly enough, that is how many days there are in a year. I decided to put my fear in God's hands because he does not want me to live in fear for the rest of my life. He told me that 365 times. It worked.

I created the thought of fear with my mind and replaced it with good thought's that God would take care of me. The fear went away. I'm back to my old self, except for my little toe. One thing you can believe is that I won't tally the next time a storm comes, I will seek shelter immediately. God gave me sense enough to react quickly, now that I'm listening to Him closely, I will be aware that the chickens can just eat later," Joanna said.

We all couldn't help laughing at the way Joanna ended her story, but what a scary thing to have happen to you. The odds of getting struck by lightening are enormous I can't even imagine the odds of being struck twice. It must be in the trillions. I think Joanna will be safe from ever being hit by lightening again in her life.

The last Diva Girl to tell a personal story is Sherry.

"If you are looking for a story as exciting as Joanna's, it's just not going to happen. Thank God nothing that exciting has ever happened to me. However I have had a life-learning event of my own.

My dad has smoked cigarettes since he was fifteen years old. He is now thirty-six years old and is having health problems due to the smoke. He is so addicted to cigarettes that he just is not able to quit on his own, so he went to the doctor for help. The doctor wrote out a prescription that would alter my dad's mind so he could stop thinking about the cigarettes all the time. The first four days, things were great. Dad put the cigarettes away and every day was a celebration. He was so happy that the addiction was lifted out of his life. Only one little pill each day and the problem was solved. He would tell my mom, 'Look at all the money we are saving, by the end of the month we will have three hundred more dollars to spend just because I don't smoke anymore.'

On the fifth day, while still on the medication, my dad asked me to run up to the lumber store with him. He was making a picnic table for the backyard. My dad was in an exceptionally good mood, joking and laughing, it was like the world was his oyster. I thought to myself, these pills my dad got from the doctor have changed his life. After the lumber was loaded on the truck, we headed for home. The lumber store is a long ways from our house and I don't even know how we got there. I wasn't watching because dad was talking to me the whole time he was driving, and I gave him my undivided attention. On our way home, a road block had been put up that wasn't there on our way to the lumbar yard, according to my dad, so we decided to take another route home, only to be stopped by another road block. Dad just stopped in front of the road block and in a panic voice said, 'They are after me honey.' I just sat quietly and watched as my dad frantically backed the truck up in an emotionally desperate attempt to get away from whoever is after us. His rapid, disordered nervous action had me on high alert. My dad had an insane look on his face that gave me a cold chill. He said to me, "Sherry, take a deep breath, I'm going to get us out of this awful situation." He than floored the gas petal and my body was sucked into the seat of the truck. I never knew the truck could move like that. Who would ever thought my dad could lay rubber. The smell of burnt rubber filled the cab of the truck as we flew down the road. I could see ahead we were running out of paved road and would soon be on a dirt road. I said to my dad 'please slow down that dirt road up ahead looks bumpy.' Dad said, "We can't afford to slow down we got to keep way ahead of them, we can't let them catch up with us."

I just closed my eyes as we merged on to the dirt road. My body felt like a rag doll as I bounced in every direction. The truck was fish tailing and I just knew any minute we were going to roll off the road.

Dad said, "Look Sherry there is a old farm house with a barn. Will pull behind that barn and wait for them to pass and then backtrack towards our house."

I said, "Who are they?"

Dad said, "Them."

We got out of the truck and peeked at the road. We must

have been there for ten minutes when the owner of the house approached us and asked if he could help. It was as if my dad snapped back to reality. He apologized to the gentleman for being on his property and explained he thought someone was chasing him. We got back in the truck and dad began to apologize for the scary experience. "I don't know what came over me, it was so real," Dad said.

When we got home dad sat down at the kitchen table and mom joined him. I went into the living room and lay down on the couch. Dad was rubbing his head while telling my mom all the details of our experience. Mom immediately called the doctor and he instructed her to flush the pills down the toilet. The doctor told mom that one in a hundred have adverse side effects from the medication. I said to myself, 'Thank God it is the medication, I thought my dad had lost it.'

In a couple of days dad was just fine and also quit smoking. The four days without a cigarette got the nicotine out of his system, just the help he needed. He told us he was just going to man up and put them down. He just didn't want to take another chance on medication having another bad reaction on him.

Everything worked out okay in the end, and I learned a valuable lesson," Sherry said.

"Let's give ourselves a hand everyone for a very interesting evening," Jan said.

It's time now to just enjoy the night sky. The stars are bright and there is not a cloud in the sky. The darker the night, the brighter the stars, and because we are far away from the city, the stars are the brightest I've ever seen. Right now I'm looking at the Big Dipper, sometimes referred to as The Great Bear. It is the pattern formed by the seven stars Alpha, Beta, Gamma, Delta, Epsilon, Zeta and Eta. Sounds like a collage sorority, a social club for women. The Little Dipper, also referred to as, The Little Bear is a northern constellation that contains the north celestial pole. It also has seven stars, and right this minute I'm enjoying it's beauty.

The universe is the most interesting subject ever. I have trouble wrapping my mind around the fact that it is continually expanding, and is referred to as the accelerating universe. In the late 1990's astronomers came to the conclusion that the universe began to accelerate about 5 billion years ago. They claim that dark energy became greater than the power of gravity that holds back the expansion. I think we will be okay in our lifetime, but I wonder what will happen way in the future.

In 1905 Albert Einstein proposed that E=mc2, which means energy, E, could be produced by destroying mass, m. I think this is what our Sun does and that is why it stays on fire.

Dark energy accounts for the missing mass-energy in the universe that is required to make it flat. Brightness of exploding stars can be used to calculate distance by comparing their distances with the red shifts of their home galaxies. This is how scientists can calculate how fast the universe is expanding.

Right now I'm looking at Orion's Belt. It is also called 'The Winter Triangle.' There are three bright stars forming a triangle pointing towards the red giant Aldebaran in Taurus, and the other towards Sirius, the brightest star in the Sky.

Stargazing is one of my favorite things to do, and tonight, because there is no artificial light from the city, the stars are clearer than I've ever seen them. Now I know what my father was talking about when he told me, 'Wilderness camping is a good way to get away from light pollution.'

My father is the one who taught me about the joy of star gazing, and the beauty that the sky provides. When I was nine years old my dad sat with me at the kitchen table with a piece of cardboard and nine marbles. He told me since I was nine years old it was time for me to learn about the nine planets. We started with the largest marble that was yellow and placed it in the center of the cardboard to be the sun. We cut a hole in the cardboard so it would stay in place. Next in line is Mercury and we used the smallest marble, followed by Venus, Earth, and Mars, which are all rocky planets. Right past the rocky planets lie's a ring of asteroids, called the Main Belt, we used glitter to represent the Main Belt. Next is the gas giant planet Jupiter which we used a large multi-colored marble. Next is Saturn, Uranus and than Neptune. We look at Pluto as an ice dwarf so we used a clear marble.

Mercury is only visible for a few days each month. Mercury passes directly between the Earth and the Sun about 13 times a century. It appears as a small black dot silhouetted against the disk of the Sun.

Venus is most similar to earth. The difference is that Venus has no detectable magnetic field, and spins slower than Earth. I believe life was on Venus at one time.

The full moon is one of my favorite nights of the month. I imagine all kinds of images on the surface. Most people see the man on the moon, but I see a rabbit sitting on its hind legs sideways. Anyway the Moon takes 27.32 Earth days to spin on its axis, which is the same time it takes to orbit the Earth.

Twelve men have walked on the surface of the moon and have brought back over 83816 lunar rocks.

The moon is full of high-titanium lunar glasses, and the mineral zinc. Some day mining for minerals could be just a normal thing on the moon.

The Moon's gravitation is felt most strongly on the side of Earth facing the Moon, and this pulls water in the oceans towards it. As the Earth rotates, the water sweeps over Earths surface, creating daily changes in sea levels called tides. The time of the high tide changes according to the Moons position in the sky. I find it so amazing that the Moon is responsible for moving water in our oceans.

Humans have a very high percentage of water in them and therefore the Moon has a dramatic effect on them. It puts a personality in a higher level. I believe this is when people find the person they are meant to be with and there is a poem I like that puts meaning to my thoughts that goes like this:

High Tide
I gravitate in your direction like the full moon pulls the tide.
An unspoken word we both can hear.
The long waves reverberate back and forth like shock waves
in my heart.
Am I a lunatic or just under the lunar spell.
You move me like the high tide under a full moon.

That poem says what I believe to be true. The Moon pulls together those who were meant to be together. If the personalities are a good match they should be together for a lifetime. In my opinion people get in to big of a hurry to find a mate. Life last for a long time, why not take some time to be sure you are right for each other. It will save you from a lot of sorrow in your future. Also a lot of money, divorce is costly. Just because the full moon pulled you together, doesn't mean your personalities are a match. Chemistry feels great, but chemistry and personality is a match made in heaven. Together they can stand the test of time.

A nightingale is perched high upon a branch of the tree we are sleeping under and sings a song to his brooding mate. Today I watched two shimmering blue butterfly's sharing a bluebell flower with their straw like mouth. It looked like they were sharing a blue malt, like two lovers would. This will be forged in my memory forever. I wonder if they are in love, as I fall asleep.

Chapter 6

Search Party

Fire Flies fill the air and Kale is in hot pursuit of them. He has a jar with at least twelve Fire Flies, but wants to fill the jar so it can provide light in his tent. He plans to release them in the morning after they have done their job.

Kale is so taken by the Fire Flies that he has wondered off some distance from the camp. He makes sure he can still see the campfire as he is in hot pursuit of the biggest Fire Fly he has ever seen. Just as Kale grabbed this Fire Fly, and slipped it into the jar, he saw two brightly glowing green eyes looking at him. As he backed up he tripped over his own feet. His heart was pounding out of his chest as he gathered himself to his feet, with his eyes now locked onto these glowing green eyes. It is like his body is in slow motion as he try's to lift his foot to take another step. His body is trembling with fear at what this creature might be. Is this Bigfoot, is he tracking us the whole time we are suppose to be tracking him?

Kale drops his jar of Fire Fly's and the big green eyes lock onto the jar, the two glows become one stream of light. This broke the power the creature had on Kale and he turned and began to run towards the camp. Kale began to regain control of him senses. Suddenly when Kale opened his mouth to scream his voice was coming out a little at a time until he was able to release his full voice filled with a shrill scream.

Kale's dad was the first to respond to his son's screams followed by the rest of the search party. Kale's dad grabbed him and Kale climbed into his dad's arms. "Are you okay son?" his dad asked. Kale began to cry so hard that all he could do was shake his head up and down. "What is wrong son, what happened to you, where are your Fire Flies?" his dad asked. All Kale could do was point back to the direction he came from.

The search party passed by Kale and his dad in search of what had frightened Kale to the point that he could not speak. Professor Sprinkle said, "Look, there's Kale's jar of Fire Flies." As he bent down to pick the jar up, there was a rustling in the bushes. Everyone shinned flashlights in the direction of the noise, but no one saw what the creature was. Professor Sprinkle handed Kale his jar of Fire Flies, and Kale looked up at him and said, "Thank you. Did you see it?" Professor Sprinkle just shook his head no.

As the search party headed back to the campsite, each picked up some sticks for the fire. If fire means safety than they want to keep it going tonight.

Kale climbed into his sleeping bag with his jar of Fire Flies and sat them next to his head. Amazingly they are giving off a lot of light and are a comfort to Kale. Kale's dad gave him a kiss on the cheek and assured him he would not leave his side and that he is safe. Kale closed his eyes and was fast asleep.

As Jake added wood to the fire he assured everyone that he would keep everyone safe. He pulled out a 357 handgun and said, "I'm not afraid to use this. It will stop anything that is roaming these hills. I've lived in this area all my life and seen wild hogs, coujars, and black bears, none of which can survive a bullet from this 357 hand gun."

Professor Sprinkle added to the conversation, "He's right, we have the advantage, I'll take a trained Forest Ranger with a weapon against any animal. After all the animal took off as soon as it saw Jake with his 357, now didn't it? The fire we built, will add more protection, animals of the night prefer the darkness.

I also have lived here all my life, and although I've never been on Tiger Mountain, I feel at home. I'm not afraid of what happened tonight, I'm excited at the thought that it might just be Bigfoot. In the morning we will look for footprints. The ground here is soft and whatever it was in those bushes will leave tracks. Jack is an expert in tracking and he can tell us just what was in those bushes tonight.

These big green eyes Kale talked about doesn't sound like any animal I've ever seen and that excites my soul. It could be Bigfoot. Wouldn't it be something to see prints in the morning that belong to Bigfoot? We would be making history, Bigfoot on Tiger Mountain. All of our names would be going in the book with others who have been privileged enough to see a print from Bigfoot's foot, or to see him running through the woods. Heck Kale senior, your son got to look him right in the eye, that's so exciting. Life seldom brings this much excitement into one's life, drink it up."

Everyone raised their cups in agreement and all said, 'cheers.' Two very strong emotions fill the camp, fear and excitement. Everyone tried to hide the fear part, but you can feel it in the air. Talking seems to calm everyone down and there is a lot of chatting going on. Normally after a long days walk up hills, everyone is ready to just sleep, the adrenal flowing through the camp won't let this happen for at least a couple of more hours.

Kale senior began to talk about his son, "You know my son was really frightened tonight but excited at the same time, I'm surprised he fell asleep so fast. Fear is always exaggerated when it is dark. We are here because of his passion to once again see another Bigfoot. My son is a genius, exceptional intellectual and gifted with creative power. He is only fourteen and is already in collage. Sometimes he goes with me on my job. You see I'm a geologist, which is the scientific study of the origin, history, and structure of the earth. My son is currently studying geomagnetism, which is the study of the earth's magnetic field. His interest is mainly in geomagnetic storms, which he believes the magnetic storms are caused by the great circle on the earth's surface formed by the intersection of a plane passing through the earth's center perpendicular to the axis connecting the north and south poles. This is referred to as the geomagnetic equator, and is responsible for the shifting of the center of the earth. That is why you heard so much about volcanos when he told about his encounter with Bigfoot back at the restaurant.

Kale's mother returned to Japan to take care of her business of manufacturing cloth bags, with the customer's company name on them who order bags. She would love to be here with us but there were problems at the plant that she had to address.

Kale told me he is certain what he saw tonight is a Bigfoot. The glowing green eyes are the same he saw at home in Japan. The smell also was the same foul odor he will never forget. This Bigfoot is much taller than my son's Bigfoot encounter. In the morning we must look for footprints and make a plaster casting for proof of what my son saw tonight. We must have evidence to establish what took place. It is of most importance to gather evidence. That is the only way some people will believe what happened. I'm excited about what the morning has to bring all of us here tonight."

Sunny said, "Look that must be a horned owl, its wing spread must be at least ten feet, it is beautiful against the full moon. They say an owl only weights around four pounds because they are actually all feathers. They just look huge.

Maybe what Kale saw is the eye of the owl? My twin brother Skylar seen one once and told me they have a yellow a greenish color to their eyes.

My parent named me Sunny after the most powerful object in the sky. The Sun is responsible for all living things.

Can you all tell that Skylar is my twin brother? We are not identical twins so we don't look alike, but we were born five minutes apart, and that makes us twins. I'm the oldest. That's why I call Skylar, little brother, even though he is taller then me. I'm named after the Sun and Skylar is named after the blue sky that matches his eyes. That's what mom told us. We are very close and never compete against each other. Competing drives a wedge and enclaves jealous feelings. I'm not saying we can't play a game of cards or checkers, I'm saying we don't compete at everyday life. That destroys relationships. Take for example, we both want to find Bigfoot, but if Skylar sees him, and I don't, I'll be happy for him and share in his victory.

We have been following Bigfoot sightings for the past ten years. Bigfoot gives us excitement, and just the thought of getting a glimpse of a Bigfoot keeps us joining the hunt. We both enjoy our vacation looking for a footprint or seeing him run through the fields or trees. If we keep hot on his trail we will eventually get close enough to see some evidence of his existence, that will be enough to satisfy my soul."

Skylar jumped into the conversation and began with "The hunt is awesome and the excitement of each search party adds to the fun. We feed off of others excitement, by that I mean, we feel what they feel and it is all the rush we need in life. People who have seen a Bigfoot reach emotions few people will ever experience in a lifetime. Their emotions peak while they tell their story, its just like they felt when they seen a Bigfoot. You can't get that kind of drama on the big screen at the movies or on the television. These are real stories and me, and my brother, love to watch people tell about their encounter with a Bigfoot. You can't tell me you all didn't feel Kale's emotion while he told his story about Bigfoot. I could see it in everybody's face that was in that room, they were all drinking it up. Someday Sunny and I will be telling our story of a sighting and others will be sharing our excitement.

We have never been on a hunt for Bigfoot with anyone who has seen two Bigfoot's in our life. Kale is making history and we are all sharing the moment with him. I can't wait till morning when Kale shares his story about what happened tonight.

By the way, my parent told me the greatest power comes

from the sky. Light, darkness, the changing of the seasons. Rain falls from the sky to give life to all roots inside the earth. The cycles of the sun, moon, and stars creates the changing of the seasons and the sky keeps everything grounded with its gravity. You tell me who is the most important, the Sun or the Sky?"

Professor Sprinkle began adding wood to the fire, "We need to take turns watching the fire and feeding it so the critters will stay away. I'll take first watch and will wake one of you in a couple of hours. You guys need to get some rest, morning will be here before you know it. We have a big day tomorrow," Professor Sprinkle said.

The moon is full and the stars are brilliantly bright. Everyone knows that sleep is important so the body can be strong to continue the hunt for Bigfoot, but the bright sky and the excitement of Kale seeing Bigfoot's glowing green eyes in the bushes, is making it difficult to wind down. Everyone climbed into the tents except Professor Sprinkle. He continued to add wood to the fire and found a piece that would be good to carve a shape of Bigfoot to give to Kale in the morning. This would help the time to pass and keep the boredom down.

After the first hour the figure starts to take on a shape that looks very much like a Bigfoot. All that's left is to make fingers and toes when suddenly clouds began to fill the air and a light sprinkle forced the good Professor to take refuge in his tent. He watched patiently as the slow rain began to put the fire out. One more hour, and it would be someone else's turn, to watch over the camp. With the clouds in the sky covering the moon and the stars, the professor began to get sleepy. He was going to close his eyes for just a couple minutes but it turned into several hours.

A high piercing scream filled the air and the entire camp woke with fear rushing through their bodies. The mules and horses were making all kinds of noise like they were being eaten alive. Though their thin covered tents all could see the green glowing eyes that Kale described earlier in the evening. These eyes would come and go as the creature blinked and changed positions as if to be circling the camp. The cracking of twigs and movement of the bushes became louder and louder as the creature came closer and closer. It is taller than the tent and is hovering over Sunny and Skylar's tent and its breath creates a movement of the tent. A faint outline of a huge creature has Sunny and Skylar hugging the ground. They cannot get low enough to stop the fear. A foul order like none has ever smelled, except for Kale, filled the air as the forest ranger turned on a flashlight and said, "Who's there. I'm armed with a weapon so you best show yourself."

Suddenly a high piercing sound filled the air, coming from far away, yet loud enough to make us put our hands over our ears for protection. The ground shook as the creature ran away from the campsite. We could hear branches breaking further and further away until all we could hear is silence. Each emerged from their tents until we were all in a circle, with flashlights in our hands. Kale had his jar of Fire Flies in his hand.

"That was no owl," Skylar said.

"You got that right little brother, looks like we have our own story to tell now," Sunny said.

"I must have fallen asleep, it's five o'clock in the morning. It will be daylight in an hour. No need in going back to sleep. I'm so sorry I put us at risk for harm. I'm ashamed of myself. Please forgive me," Professor Sprinkle said.

No one wanted to punish Professor Sprinkle and they all let him know his fire going out was the only reason Bigfoot came to our camp. They were thanking him, not criticizing him. Excitement filled the air as the tents were taken down and packed away. As daylight broke through the sky, Kale opened his jar of Fire Flies and thanked them for a job well done as they flew away.

The horses and mules were scattered throughout the bushes but all were okay. The rain once again began to fall lightly and the search party put things in high gear to search for a footprint.

Kale was sticking close to his dad for protection. He knew everyone believes what he saw because they all seen the same glowing green eyes Kale described.

Kale said to his dad, "Back home I was not afraid like now. I think it is because it was familiar ground. It was my territory. You know this Bigfoot is much taller than the one I seen back home. In my mind I know he is young and dumb to have gotten so close to people. Dad, I think what we seen tonight is a monster teenager Bigfoot. I think the cry we heard echoing in the mountains were the parents of this Bigfoot telling him to come home."

"Look everyone, way up high in the sky, it's an Eagle. Do you see him? Can you believe that that Eagle can see a mouse in the grass from way up there in the sky? I guess that is where the saying Eagle eye came from.

Native Americans are the only people allowed to own a feather from an Eagle. I think we are in Indian Territory right now. I know for sure that Tahlequah Oklahoma, which is down the road, is Cherokee Territory.

The Cherokee once lived in the Carolinas, Virginias, Kentucky, Tennessee, Georgia, and Alabama. They grow Maize, or Corn in the river valleys where the ground is fertile. This was their main grain. The U.S. government forced them to travel 1,000 miles to Indian Territory here in Oklahoma in 1838. This is referred to as the trail of tears on which many Cherokee people died," the forest ranger said.

Suddenly a thunderbolt launched from the sky like a furious angry creature wanting to strike fear in our hearts. Right after that we once again heard the cry of Bigfoot. His cry rang out through the hollow mountains far away from where we now stand. We all looked at each other with a great amount of satisfaction on our faces. The sun is just beginning to light the gray sky as the rain began to gently fall. We must hurry to find a print before the rain, washes them away.

All seemed magical with the cry of Bigfoot ringing through

the hills and the celestial fluids fall as rain from the heavens upon our faces. Our hearts are light with the anticipation of finding a footprint to prove to the world that Bigfoot lives in these hills as the rain falls harder and harder.

The hope of finding a print begins to fade, as we no longer can see in front of our faces because the rain is so heavy. We search for shelter and the forest ranger waves us over to a hole in the side of the hill. The chill of terror filled our souls as we entered the cave and see that it is filled with bones of animals that very well could have fed Bigfoot. Could this be Bigfoot's home?

The rain is slowing down and the sky is brightening up as the winds begin to pick up. Suddenly once again the sky darkens. Could this be a tornado? The outside of the cave is becoming as scary as the inside, the wind has trees bending down to kiss the ground and we back deeper into the cave to keep from being pulled out by the wind.

We heard a rumbling at the back of the cave but it was to dark to see what was there. Professor Sprinkle fumbled through his backpack looking for his flashlight. The forest ranger had his gun pulled ready to fire, pointed in the direction of the noise.

Kale's voice broken with sobs, and tears flowing down his face said, "Dad please, do not let them shoot Bigfoot. He will be more afraid of us than we are of him. If we all stand to the side, I know he will just run out of the cave away from us. I don't see any human bones in here. Bigfoot is just sustaining himself on wild game he hunted down and devoured for nourishment. Look this is the bone of a deer, and this looks like a squirrel. Please don't let them hurt Bigfoot."

As professor Sprinkle fumbled through his backpack he finally found his flashlight, he pointed it in the direction of the noise. A large black bear, raises up on his hind feet, and with his mouth open let out a earth shattering roar. His teeth looked to be at least an inch long and his eyes as wild as anything any of us have ever seen. Everyone turned and ran out of the cave into the blowing rain. Fear filled our bodies as we ran back down the mountain. Lucky for us the bear just wanted us out of his home. He did not follow.

Soaked to the bone and stupefied with terror we hurried down the hills. The rain is subsiding and the winds are now less strong. The forest ranger got on his two-way radio and requested four wheelers to meet us at a certain point to take us back to town. Our mules and horses have already headed for home and left us behind.

The forest ranger is at the back of the line looking over his shoulder regularly to be sure the bear is not following the search party. The forest ranger hollers out to Professor Sprinkle, who is leading the group, "I think we can take a break now, the bear never left the cave."

We are all breathing hard and welcome the break. There is a sadness in the air, we all want proof of what we seen, a footprint cast in Plaster of Paris. The rain has destroyed any hope of that. What we do have is our story of a pair of green glowing eyes on a twelve-foot creature that was in the bushes. We all seen these eyes, smelled him, and heard the branches breaking as he fled away. We all heard the shrill cry's of the distant Bigfoot calling our Bigfoot to come home. We are not empty handed. We have our story of what we seen and heard, a family of Bigfoot's. We are witnesses for each other.

Chapter 7

Footprint

Sparks and cinders rose from the campfire as the cries of Bigfoot echoes in the mountains. I was blinded, by my tears of fear as the night's falling shadows, hide the day, and my half shut eyes, in a half dream state have me falling asleep.

The gentle rain is slowly putting out the campfire and the Diva Girls put their fears to rest, of the cry of Bigfoot that echoes as the fire is diminishing. Everything went silent except the beating of my heart that keeps thumping in my ears. When the moon was once again overhead we could again see a calm reflection in the night sky.

The dew is so heavy I seem to be drinking the morning air. Thoughts of Bigfoot enter my mind and I wonder why most people disbelieve generally the existence of the Bigfoot. If they could hear what we heard last night they would have to acknowledge Bigfoot's existence. It was the cry of a wild human, a Bigfoot.

As I look across the hills, I can see the area where the search party is camped and rain is falling. It is dark as night on that hill. It's funny how rain can fall from the sky in one place and the sun be shinning in another just a little ways apart. I wonder if the search party is all wet.

Bigfoot was on every Diva Girl's mind and he was the top subject around the breakfast table. One of the Diva Girl's named Rachel said, "I wonder what Bigfoot is having for breakfast this morning." Crystal immediately responded with, "I image the fierce savage Bigfoot is feeding veraciously on his hunted prey a deer. This monster human is cruelty eating this deer alive this very moment." Jan the Diva leader interrupted, "That's enough Crystal, you are ruining the girls appetite. We have a long day ahead of us and need the food for energy."

After breakfast we headed for the blue butterflies to capture the magic on film. I found one sunning itself on a brown rock, wings fully spread looking like the perfect picture. The contrast of the rock brought out the brilliant color of the blue wings and yellow spotted body. This is my perfect picture. As I hunt for another unusually shot, I find a blue butterfly hanging upside down on the branch of a tree with it's legs and head in full sight. As I snap its picture, this butterfly looks right into the camera like it was posing for a picture. I didn't even have to say, cheese.

Occasionally I look up at the sides of the mountain to see if I can get a glimpse of Bigfoot. My dream was so real-like that I feel connected to Bigfoot. I'm on fire with the love of adventure even though Bigfoot has eluded our pursuit and was out of danger of being discovered by the Diva Girl's, maybe the search party headed by Professor Sprinkle seen Bigfoot, up close.

In every group you have the doubters. Some of the girls believe what we saw was a red deer, yet they can't explain what we heard in the night, Bigfoot's cry. No one ever heard that sound before.

The summer sun has created an explosion of plant life on the other side of the hill from where the butterflies are. The vines look like lace draped across the limbs of the tree. Crystal noticed I stopped dead in my track and asked, "What's wrong." I reached out my hand towards the vines that ranged from lime green to a green so dark it looked almost black. They were intertwined and made themselves look magical. Crystal said, "That is the most beautiful thing I've ever seen. Let's walk inside and take some pictures.

It's a great background. It's more beautiful than any artist could ever paint, except for the dead deer."

"You know Crystal, my father always told me that nature is indifferent to the cruel fate of animals, this is hard for humans to relate to, it is cruel to them, but it is nature at it's finest. It is just the way things are meant to be," I said.

This is what animals do they eat each other for dinner. We are the highest on the food chain and we eat animals. We just don't think about it because they are cut up and put in a package. When we make a hamburger patty, we don't think about the cow it came from. We just make it nice and round and flat and throw it on the grill to cook.

Crystal was shaking and rubbing her shoes on the grass to get any part of the deer off of her shoes. There was only a little hair on the side of her shoe, but she was freaking out about the whole thing. She was squeamishly moving around like she had bugs in her britches.

"Crystal it's okay. Calm down, everyone is looking at you like you are some kind of a spastic nut," I said.

Jan and some of the girls were coming in our direction. Crystal finally got her composure back as they approached. Jan Said, "What is wrong, girls?" Crystal pointed in the direction of the vines. Jan said, "That's so beautiful. It looks like a fairy tale land."

Crystal said, "Yes it is beautiful but just the other side of that log is a dead animal."

Jan instructed the girls to stay back as she and the forest ranger went to investigate what was behind the log. Sure enough, it is a dead deer. It is very freshly killed for the blood is still bright red. "Whatever killed this deer took its hind legs with it. All the meat was taken off the ribs like it was eaten in place," Jan said. Jan took pictures of the deer to report back to the base camp in case it needed looking into.

Jan said, "Okay girls let's get back to taking pictures of blue butterflies, it looks like a storm is moving in and we will shortly be heading back down the mountain. You have five minutes to finish taking pictures."

Everyone was talking about Bigfoot having lunch right there in the woods. One of the girls said, "We should have asked him to join us." Everyone got a laugh out of that. Crystal said, "It's not funny, I stepped on that dead animal and I know I will have nightmares about it for some time. Joanna, one of the Diva Girls said, "Crystal, don't have such a pessimistic assessment of human nature, we are just trying to make light of the situation so you can get over it. I now realize that your individual emotional capacity to make fun of your fears needs some work." Crystal responded with, "Humans are naturally good and it shows in their emotional responses to pain and suffering of a fellow human being, it's called being compassionate, something you are lacking in Joanna. Maybe you should go live with Bigfoot. You have more in common with him than you do with humans."

Joanna responded with, "In case you haven't been informed, Bigfoot is a human being, and I think he would be a pretty cool human being."

About that time Jan came into the circle of girls and said, "There is lightening to the south of us and we must put it in high gear and get off this mountain. Be ready to go in two minutes."

As we headed down the mountain in a single file, an every so light rain began to fall. It was refreshing and I lifted my face to the heavens and opened my mouth to taste it. Most of the girls were going through their back packs looking for their rain coats, I had mine tied around my waist, and when I feel the need to put it on, I will. Right now I'm enjoying the freshness of the smell of rain. I thought to myself, if I ever had the chance to invent a perfume, it would smell like rain.

Suddenly the wind began to pick up and the trees looked like they were kissing the ground. Jan's eyes are wide with apprehension as she told us to get down in a gully and put our hands over our heads and roll up into a ball. The sky was turning black and the wind now sounds like a train over our heads. When the lightening would strike, it lit up the sky, and it is like a horror movie, terror filled the air. Thunder filled the air and there was a roaring heard in the earth, the trees began to shake and lightening once again split the sky open. A stroke of lightening shattered the trunk of a tree and the splitting of its trunk was deafening. The tree fell across the gully we are in. I could hear many of the Diva Girl's sobbing. Jan kept saying, "Everything going to be okay, just keep your heads down."

The rain is now pouring down like buckets of water being poured over us. The gully is holding water and thoughts of it filling up, and all of us drowning passes through my mind. I quickly dismiss the thought realizing a frenzied state of mind can get me hurt. I gather my thoughts and move slowly to higher ground, staying low. As I turn to look over my shoulder, I see everyone following right behind me. Just as we reached a ledge to safety, the rain stops, the clouds clear and it was as if nothing even happened except for the trees that were struck by lightening laying all over the place.

We all got to our feet and began hugging each other. Jan said, "Is everyone alright." She began to call everyone's name until the last Diva Girl said, "Here."

Jan asked if we wanted her to call for help to get us down from Tiger Mountain and all the Diva Girls said in unison, "No." We are a very independent group of girls, and the whether is great now.

Some of the trails we are taking are very slippery and we tend to fall occasionally. I don't think I've ever been this dirty in my entire life. The rain has made it where you slip down before you even know your falling. It's a good thing we are going down hill. We had more fun going down this mountain laughing at each others inability to keep a footing, than anything else on the whole trip.

Crystal had to relieve herself and could not hold it another minute. We always go in two's when such an emergency occurs. I gave Jan a howler for we always let her know when we take a break from the group, and she howler back, "Thank you, we will wait for you."

While Crystal took care of her business I noticed an

impression in the mud. It looked like a giant footprint. I immediately pulled out my camera and began taking pictures. Crystal joined me shortly and gave out a cry, "It's Bigfoot." I continued taking pictures from every angle while Crystal ran to tell everyone what we found. She was screaming at the top of her voice, "It's Bigfoot, It's Bigfoot, we found a footprint."

As Crystal brought the group to the footprint she said, "Stay away from over there, that's where my emergency stop is." Everyone gathered around the print and began taking pictures. Crystal put her foot next to the Bigfoot print to show the size difference.

Jan said, "Girls we are making history today. Our names are going down in the books that record Bigfoot's existence. Do you all have any idea what this means."

Jan tried calling back to base camp but something is wrong with the two-way radio. She can't get an answer.

"Girls we must leave markers so we can find this print again and make a Plaster of Paris molding to prove to the world we found Bigfoot's footprint. Get out your hair bands and dirty socks. I'll tie them to branches on the trees so we can get back to this spot without any trouble. After a while these woods all look the same. We need markers to get us back to this very spot," Jan said.

Jan looped the headbands around tree limbs, and tied our socks to other tree limbs, every ten feet or so. We should not have any problems finding our way back to Bigfoot's footprint with these markers.

When we came to a ledge big enough and flat enough to take a break, we decided to have lunch. We are all so dirty that everyone decided to just eat trail mix, we could pour it in our mouths from the package and never touch it with our dirty hands. We are just a couple of hours away from our base camp and the trail mix will hold us until then.

Everyone is talking about the size of the footprint. We take turns guessing on the size of the print. Numbers are being thrown around from size fifteen inches to twenty inches long and eight to twelve inches wide. We are all super excited that we found Bigfoot's print.

Jan said, "Break is over, let's get down this mountain and let the world know about Bigfoot's footprint. The quicker we get to base camp the sooner we will all get a shower. My hair is so nasty I can't hardly wait to shower, so let's get a head count and get moving."

Parts of the trail go straight down and we just sit on our bottoms and slide down, it's better than risking a stumble, and rolling down the hill head first, and breaking our nose or something like that. At least we have some control, the heavy rain earlier has the ground as slick as snot.

Jan is leading the group and lets us know when she comes across a dangerously slick spot. She gives everyone a holler, "I'm going for a slide," On the really rough trails she made a pad for our butts. She filled her back pack with leaves and tied a rope to the strap, than to a tree, so when she gets to the bottom of the hill the next Diva Girl in line can pull the rope with the backpack up the hill and take their ride down with ease. The last one unties the rope and rides the backpack to safety. It would really hurt if you hit a rock with your butt while sliding down a trail. Jan is the best Diva Girl leader we could have leading us, she takes great safety measures with her Diva Girls.

The hill we are facing now is the hardest hill to go down yet. We remember what a difficult time it was going up, so we know what we are up against. It swerves and curves and we completely lose sight of Jan after the first curve. She is talking to us all the way down and letting us know we can all do this. When Jan got to the bottom of the most difficult hill, we have to tackle today, she gave us a shout out, " Use your feet to slow yourself down. When you girls get down here I have something to show you."

We all looked at each other wide eyed with excitement at what Jan had to show us. Crystal said, "Do you think she has Bigfoot?" Everyone gave a chuckle, like, yah right.

Jan waited until everyone made it down the trail safely

and then unwrapped the most beautiful baby Eagle. It has a powerful looking hooked bill and long claws on its feet. Its eyes are as yellow as the sun and its head is white as a cloud. It looked up at us with its mouth wide open like it was hungry.

Jan said, "It must have fallen out of the nest during the storm. Its wings are all wet and heavy with mud. We need to get him off this hill and into a wildlife refuge. They will know how to get him back into good shape and old enough to make it in the wild. The Eagle is a protected bird and girls, few people have ever gotten this close to an Eagle." After she said that, everyone pulled out their cameras and began taking pictures. Jan let each of us touch its head.

After we all get our eyes full of this Eagle, Jan wrapped it back up to keep it dry and warm. This Eagle warms my heart, and I'm excited that I was able to get this close to an Eagle. People just don't get the opportunity to touch an Eagle and see a footprint of Bigfoot in the same day. I feel so lucky right now.

As we continued down the trail, Crystal noticed a group of worms crawling on the side of the trail and she gave a shout to Jan, "We have some worms here, on the side of this trail, do you think the Eagle would like one for lunch." As I bent down to look at these worms I noticed they were not worms, but they were baby snakes. I stepped on a couple of them because I didn't want to pick up live snakes. By the time Jan got to the spot where we are, I had two held up for her to see. "Oh snakes, that is perfect for this little guy," Jan said. She gently unwrapped the eagle and I held the baby snakes up for him to devour. It took just a minute for him to focus but when he realized it was food he reached up and grabbed the snake by the tail. I made sure he couldn't reach my finger for he would try to eat it also. One wasn't enough. The baby Eagle was crawling out of his warm place to get this second snake. I stepped on a couple of more of these snakes and four was enough for the baby Eagle. On the last one, he wasn't crawling out of his warm spot to eat, that's how I knew he had enough. If it were legal for me to raise this Eagle I would try talking Jan into letting me have him. Jan wrapped him back up and we were once again on our way to base camp.

Chapter 8

Base Camp

We were only an hour away from base camp when a group of people calling themselves the, 'rescue team,' were talking to Jan and the forest ranger. We could hear Jan telling them we were all just fine, that our two-way radios just stopped working during an electrical storm. She talked about how she thought the storm fried the radios when the lightening struck the tree. Jan unwrapped the Eagle and showed it to the rescue team, they were giving all kinds of ah, ah, ahs.

The rescue team began passing out bottled water and it was well received by all. One of the rescue team members said, "You all are a mess, I bet you will welcome a hot shower." Everyone was in agreement, that is a good idea.

The captain of the rescue team began telling Jan that the search party that is looking for Bigfoot also had a rescue team helping them back to base camp. Jan is telling the captain about the footprint we seen and the captain suggested they get a Plaster of Paris kit and get up their as soon as we were all safe.

We could make it back to base camp by ourselves but it was nice to have a cold bottle of water and some company. If something bad did happen to one of us, its nice to know someone would rescue us.

We were back to base camp before we knew it. I took the longest shower of my entire life. The mud was packed under my fingernails and I had to use a brush to get all of it out.

After getting all cleaned up the first thing I wanted to do was visit the baby Eagle. I gave him a nickname, 'fuzzy head,' he has white fuzz on his head instead of feathers. The feathers grow only after they are a few months old. Jan put fuzzy head in a cage with a light on one end to help dry his feathers. He seems right at home under the warm light, I guess it's like being under his mothers feathers.

The rescue team and the forest rangers are gathering under a tree to discuss where the Bigfoot footprint is located so they can get a Plaster of Paris molding. I can hear some of what they are saying, like 'It is going to be very slippery trying to go up that trail. We will need lots of rope to throw around trees to pull ourselves up the slick hills.' One of the forest rangers said, "I have a better idea, let's have the helicopter lower us where we think the footprint is, that would be a lot safer." Everyone clapped their hands at the great idea and before they knew it they were up in the air and on their way to ensure that a Plaster of Paris mold would prove the existence of Bigfoot on Tiger Mountain.

The human species is about 350,000 years old and we are hunters and gathers of what nature provides. We are the same as Bigfoot only we have lost many of the skills that Bigfoot has for survival value. We now depend on a few farmers to plant what winds up on the grocery shelves, and we depend on a few butchers to cut up the meat we eat. Would we even be able to survive, without the grocery store around the corner from our house? If there were to be a catastrophic event, how many families would become extinct, no longer existing, because they don't know how to till the soil to raise plants to eat, or they don't know how to kill an animal for food, my guess is more than half the families would become extinct. They just would not have the skill sets to survive. Extinction is a natural process caused by nature, but nature has a resiliency to re-invent itself, if people have the skill to survive. We live in the lost age of harmony with nature, something Bigfoot has mastered. Humans are burdened with a consciousness which brings about shame, guilt, and regret that can consume the mind to the breaking point when it comes to killing an animal.

Bigfoot doesn't live in a political correct world. He lives in the world of nature. I would say his motto is, 'live smart, die old.' Political correctness has a place in this world of ours, it is for humans, political correctness doesn't belong in nature.

The helicopter is lifting into the air and we watch as it disappears behind the trees. Excitement fills the air knowing soon we will have proof that Bigfoot lives on Tiger Mountain. The footprint cast in Plaster of Paris is the proof that can't be denied.

We have our pictures of what we think is Bigfoot far away on the opposite hill we were climbing for proof. What we seen was red haired much like what Scottie described. Some of the girls thought it was just a deer, but once they seen the footprint they were also convinced it was Bigfoot.

The pictures of the footprint turned out great. There is no denying the size when compared to a normal size foot, which we had beside it, when the picture was snapped.

The team, searching for the footprint were hovering over a clearing that was close to where the forest ranger felt the footprint was and each was lowered one at a time. The helicopter was holding steady even though the wind was still brisk. All were in hopes that the drizzle of rain had not melted the print. To ease their fear the forest ranger said, "The print is deep enough that it should be okay."

As the team located the trail the Diva Girls were on when they found the footprint, everything looked the same. It was like a needle in a haystack. The team felt they were in the general area but there was no sign of the headbands and socks. They decided to backtrack on the trail they just finished covering to look for any signs they might have missed. They were certain they were in the right location. A broken twig got the forest rangers attention, than another, and another. Something removed all the headbands and socks off the limbs of the trees. The team now is following broken twigs all the way to the footprint. Everyone gave a gasp at the sight of the size of the footprint.

The footprint is half full of water and the team must empty it before they can make a mold. In their backpacks each has a spoon to dip the water out. As they remove the water there is talk about the disappearance of the hair bands and socks that Jan had tied to the tree limbs. Some thought Bigfoot took them just because they were there. Others thought he took them because they belonged to humans. That is why Scottie and Kale had an encounter with him. Bigfoot is curious about humans.

The water is removed and the Plaster of Paris is ready to be poured. The process takes time and in order to protect the footprint, the team decides to cover the print with a tent, in case the rain starts again. Once the tent is in place the Plaster of Paris is poured. The team now spreads out in search of another print. Everyone is in agreement that Bigfoot returned and gathered up all the headbands and socks the Diva Girls left behind, so there must be other prints somewhere.

The forest ranger gave out a shout, "Over here, I found what looks like a smudged footprint." Everyone quickly joined the forest ranger and all agreed it was from Bigfoot only it is on the side of a slope and is more like a smudge than a print. Everyone got out their cameras and began taking pictures. No need to do a Plaster of Paris, its not a definable print.

"Let's see how far the trail takes us," said the forest ranger. In a single file the team started up the steep hill. There is no trail to follow, just a hunch, a guess, and the ground is covered in leaves. The team kept a keen eye for something that looked out of place. A broken twig, leaves that looked to be crushed, would be a sign that Bigfoot is going in that direction.

The hill is straight up now and the team must throw ropes around tree trunks to pull themselves up the hill. They have a three-hour window to find another print, by then nightfall will set in.

After an hour of climbing the hills the team reached a plateau that had bluebells and Butterflies as far as the eye can see. The forest ranger said, "The Diva Girls will love this place." Looking around for smashed plants, the team puts distance between themselves. If they can find a trail of smashed plants, they can document the direction to Bigfoot's home.

The bluebells, with a glorious shimmer in the evening sun, have everybody looking at them with amazement. The whole team began snapping pictures to show the base camp the beauty they discovered. There are thousands of blue butterflies floating in the air and hanging by a leg or two on the bluebell flowers. This is a piece of heaven on earth.

Everyone searched for a sign of Bigfoot's presence, but none was found. Nightfall is creeping in and all are in agreement that it's time to head for base camp. Bigfoot once again has eluded being photographed up close and personal.

The team lowered themselves down the hill with the help of ropes. Going down is much faster and a lot less work. The Plaster of Paris should be dry by now.

When the team reaches the spot where the tent and Plaster of Paris is suppose to be, there was nothing. Bigfoot must have taken them. The print is disturbed to the point it is just a smudge. This Bigfoot is obsessed with human treasures. The whole time the team was in pursuit of Bigfoot, he was just waiting for the right moment to gather the goods. He is very smart, after all he is a human being with higher senses. No one to this day has captured a Bigfoot or found the remains, the bones, of a Bigfoot. That says a lot for the intelligence of Bigfoot.

The team now is filled with disappointment and no proof of what was found on Tiger Mountain other than photos. The silence is like a sadness, a dark moment for each involved. Bigfoot snatched the evidence right out of their hands. Each knew what they saw, a fifteen inch footprint, but when they try to tell others about it, will they be believable without proof.

Yes, each will tell their story about what happened on Tiger Mountain today, but how many people can they convince about what actually happened. Will they feel the skepticism in the people that they share the story with?

Hard evidence makes things much easier to talk about. It gives confidence to even those that don't have the gift of gab. Being able to hold up a Plaster of Paris fifteen-inch footprint grabs an audience full attention.

The Diva Girls who found the print counted on the team to bring back the evidence. Will they have the confidence to tell their story without proof?

Chapter 9

Evening News

Reporters from three different news channels arrived before the Plaster of Paris team even made it back to base camp. Each, reporter is patiently awaiting the return of the evidence, of a Bigfoot footprint.

They have already started interviewing Kale, Scottie and the Diva Girls. Crystal suggested we get our film developed at the one-hour developing department, and the pictures turned out great. The picture of Bigfoot, on the opposite hill from where the Diva Girls were, showed something that was red haired but the news team wasn't sure if it was a red deer or maybe even a bear. They suggested we get some experts to blow up the pictures and magnify the red spot to see if indeed it is Bigfoot. If we have a shot of his face in any of these pictures we will all be famous.

The news people were very impressed with the pictures of the footprint and excitement was in the air that soon a Plaster of Paris print would be coming down Tiger Mountain for all to see.

People are pitching tents all around the base camp hoping to see all the evidence of a Bigfoot sighting first hand. Every Hotel and Motel is full in a fifty-mile radius and there must be a hundred cars parked on the side of the road. The police were called in to help direct traffic and keep the peace. Right now base camp is vibrating with excitement.

Native American Cherokee's have set up a teepee and plan to stay and protect Bigfoot from being exploited. My dad is a good friend with some of the Indian leaders and I recognized one and said, 'hello.' He invited me to join the Cherokee's in the tent, and I felt honored. "I want you all to meet Chelsea Songbird, her dad is a good friend of mine. I asked her to join us," said Rick Foxfire.

We sat in the teepee and listened to the Indian leaders talk about ancient stories of Bigfoot in a 'council ceremony,' with a fire pit burning sage and dill that filled our senses. We are learning to achieve harmony with nature, very much like what Bigfoot has found.

Rick Foxfire said, "Bigfoot is a friend to the Cherokee people even though we have never talked to him. We know he lives in these hills and we are here to protect him from exploitation. The value of a friend is when he is closer than a brother or sister. The lifeline of a friendship, is mutual confidence, you can trust one another. Friendship is a two way street, both must be able to share feelings, at a distance. Bigfoot is all of that.

How do you disprove what many have seen with their own eyes? You cannot. No one has ever talked to Bigfoot, yet we feel his presence in these hills. We can hear him and feel the power in his voice. It may only be a yell, but when we hear it, we tremble at his unique sound that has no equal or rival. That yell belongs to a human being, not just another animal it belongs to a Bigfoot. My heart is penetrated by the mystery of his elusiveness, and the sounds of his cry's.

Knowing the history of mankind will let you know what they are capable of doing. Take heed to the knowledge you gain by exploring history and avoid the evil that control creates. Bigfoot must not be controlled my man, it is crucial to his future.

Through my imagination of who Bigfoot is, I have reached a higher emotion of what Bigfoot's friendship would mean to me. Bigfoot cannot live under the man made law, he will perish.

We are here today to protect the rights of our friend

Bigfoot. Dignity of the individual is acquired through the inalienable rights of the human and Bigfoot is human. The most important freedom of all is the freedom of our minds and Bigfoot must be allowed to live the life nature provides. He will perish if captured, and put in a cage like an animal."

I enjoyed being part of the conversation that my dad's friend shared in the teepee. I agree with every word he said. It made me think about what would happen to Bigfoot if he were captured. I image his sad face behind bars. What would the people who captured him do with him? Would they indeed put him in a cage and do experiments on him?

When I came out of the teepee, I saw a reporter interviewing Kale. Kale was saying, "The smell of Bigfoot was so vivid that I seemed to be transported across time and space to be back in Japan where I first seen Bigfoot. The eyes are just like Scottie described them, glowing green, like a haze is coming off them. The pupil of his eye is round. This is how I know he is human. I believe this Bigfoot and the one back home are monster Bigfoot teenagers. This is why he has gotten so close to me, and Scottie. We are both teenagers and he is curious about people his own age. No Bigfoot has ever gotten this close to a human in history. Teenagers are notorious for getting into trouble. I just bet his parents are not very happy with him right now."

Kale has a charismatic charming way about him and right now he has the news reporters eating out of the palm of his hand. While listening to Kale talk about Bigfoot being a teenager, I gained clarity with a new perspective on Bigfoot's family. For some reason I always thought of Bigfoot in a singular mode.

After Kale talked about the Bigfoot he saw, being a teenager, I started thinking about what my mother tells me about teenagers all the time. She tells me that the frontal lobes are responsible for reasoning and problem solving and they start developing rapidly during the teenage years, this is why most teens don't think things through or consider the outcome of their actions. Their frontal lobes are all over the place, and they forget to consider the consequences of their actions. If teens know the frontal lobes are causing all the recklessness that is going on in their life, maybe they will deal with situations differently. I think Kale is spot on about this Bigfoot being a teenager. This is the only Bigfoot that has been reckless enough to get this close to people. Also, he got close to Scottie and Kale who are both teenagers. Oh let's don't forget Kale saw a teenage Bigfoot in Japan. I wonder how many other young people have seen Bigfoot and their parents thought it was just their imagination, and disregarded what their children told them?

Crystal is being interviewed and she is saying, "My body filled with a sense of melancholy as I gazed upon the atrocious deed's of what Bigfoot had done to this disfigured deer that lay before me. I climbed a hill, and gazing through the woods, I found no habitation that could have done such a thing, this is when I was sure what I had seen was the leftovers of Bigfoot's lunch.

As I climbed the side of the mountain, the winds became strong and a storm of thunder and lightening ensued."

Crystal continued her drama filled story until the reporter finally said, "Thank you very much."

Chapter 10

Return of the Search Party

As the team neared the base camp they could see all the cars lining the street, and tents, which were everywhere. The forest ranger said, "Looks like we have a fan club down there. They will be disappointed when they see we are empty handed. Everyone is here to see the Plaster of Pairs footprint, and all we have is a story to tell them about how it disappeared."

Someone must have got a glimpse of the team, for all were heading to the foot of the hill. Its like Bigfoot is a rock star and his groupies want to be there for him.

The police officers gather at the front of the crowd and begin talking into a bullhorn. The officer said, "We will all get to see what is coming down the hill so be patient. We need to keep the evidence safe. Give the team plenty of room."

Disappointment filled the air when everyone seen the team was empty handed. The forest ranger told his story and the crowd was spellbound by each event told. All are convinced Bigfoot is somewhere on Tiger Mountain, and he is watching everything that is going on.

I wanted to find Scottie in this crowd of people to share my enthusiasm about Bigfoot. It took an hour to find him and then I had to get permission from his parents to talk with him. They are very protective of Scottie. I told them that I wrote a poem for Scottie and I would like to read it to him. First, they read the poem, and then introduced me to Scottie. I said to Scottie, "Bigfoot has widespread fame here on Tiger Mountain thanks to you, and I have prepared a poem in celebration of his sighting. It goes like this:

Teenage Bigfoot

You elude me like a lightening flash disappears in the sky on a stormy night.
Your reflection in the glassy cool translucent stream sends shock waves through my brain.
I got an injection of oxygen with a glimpse as you climb the narrow gorge.
I'm so jazzed that I got, eye-to-eye contact, with your green glowing eyes.
Are you a lonely teenager, loneliness is the saddest state of existence.
Friendship is the only thing that can cure loneliness, are you starving for a friend?
As you perch on the neighboring cliff, is your yell full of sorrow, dark and deep with pain.
If so, I'll summon up some courage and put aside my horror-struck fears, and be your friend.
There is certain fluidity in your yell, full of deep emotions.
I'm amped up about our memorable moment when you passed over me like a silent shadow.
Tears of joy are in my eyes, as I realize your loneliness, I now know your personal pain could only mean my gain.
You shared your emptiness, now let me end your search for a teenage friend."

"Chelsea Songbird, that is the nicest thing anyone has ever done for me. You have opened my eyes to the fact that Bigfoot is a teenager just like us. This has changed my way of thinking. Fear has been lifted from my heart and replace with a warm fuzzy feeling. I feel connected to Bigfoot now that I know he is a lonely teenager. No one can understand this except another lonely teenager like myself.

I'm meeting with Kale in a couple of hours to compare what we have both seen, those glowing green eyes. No other creature on earth can claim those eyes. I know this in my heart.

Chelsea would you like to come over and meet Kale. I would like to share your poem with Kale," Scottie said.

"I would love to meet Kale and share your poem, this is yours, but I will be happy to read it for you.

If it is alright with you I would like to bring my friend Crystal who was with me when I stumbled onto Bigfoot's footprint," I said.

"Sure the more the merrier, and thank you again for my poem, and I would love for you to read it to Kale," Scottie said.

As I left the cabin that Scottie and his parents are staying in, a sense of pleasure filled my body. I want to call it accomplishment. I did something so profound with my words, I took away fear from a young persons heart. Word's really do matter. The fear left Scottie as quickly as it consumed him. I could see it in his eyes as I glanced at him while reading his poem. He now knows that Bigfoot wanted to be his friend. At least that is what he thinks now. Fear is just a state of mind that we create. I can't say that I blame Scottie for filling his mind with fear, but it would be an awful way to spend one's life. My words are mighty powerful to have chased away that fear. I feel good that I was able to lift fear from Scottie's heart and mind.

When I got back to the Diva Girl cabin, Crystal met me at the door. "What is he like, is he handsome, did you like his personality, is he a jock or a prep?" Crystal said.

"First of all he is very nice and handsome, and he is an intellectual, very smart, and he invited you to come with me tonight to meet him and Kale. He loved the poem I wrote for him and he told me that it made him realize Bigfoot is just a lonely teenager looking for a friend. With that awareness his fears of Bigfoot left his mind, like when a shade is lifted from a window and light fills the room. That really made me feel, very good to have made a difference in his life. We better take our showers and fix our hair. This is like going on a date. I'm so excited," I said.

After we took our showers, combed our hair, and got dressed, Crystal said, "If I knew I would be going on my first date I would have brought my curling iron, maybe even some makeup and lipstick."

"Come on now Crystal, you may own a curling iron but I know you don't have makeup or lipstick yet, your only fourteen years old, way to young to be painting your face," I said.

"Your right I don't have any makeup, but if I did, I would make myself up to be real pretty. After all this is my first date ever," Crystal said.

"You know I was only kidding when I said it is like going on a date. Scottie just wants to talk about Bigfoot. He knows we seen something that is red on the opposite hill from where we were climbing and wants to talk about it. He also knows we seen the footprint and wants to see the pictures that we have. This is strictly about Bigfoot, but if we want to have fun and pretend it is our first date, we can do that. Remember, it is just pretend," I said.

As we got close to Scottie's door, our pretending to be on a date had us all up in the air. The mind is an amazing tool, what we think defiantly controls how we act. We both need to get control of ourselves before we knock on the door. I would be embarrassed if Scottie and Kale seen, me and Crystal, all giggle like we are right now.

"Okay Crystal, take a deep breath, and come back to reality. I'm going to knock on Scotties door now," I said.

Scottie's mom answered the door and introduced herself to Crystal, and gave me a hug. It felt like I've been her friend all my life. What my poem did for Scottie has her grateful and she shows her gratitude.

"Can I get you girls anything to drink?" Scottie's mom said.

We both asked for a glass of water. On the table there is chips and dip, squares of cheese, and rolled up slices of ham and turkey. I thought to myself, 'how nice.'

Scottie said, "Have a seat girls, this is Kale."

"This is my friend Crystal, and Crystal this is Scottie," I said.

Now that everyone knows each other we can get down to business, exchanging events concerning Bigfoot. When we showed our pictures of Bigfoot's footprint with a normal size shoe beside it, Scottie and Kale got real excited. We told how all the Diva Girls donated their extra socks and hair bands to tie on tree limbs so we could find the print when we returned.

"You know that the search party that went back up the hill, they never found our socks or hair bands. Bigfoot must have taken all the socks to wear on his toe's, and with all that hair he could have fifteen pony tails with our hair bands." Crystal said.

We all got a kick out of Crystal's sense of humor. Scottie and Kale are both very intelligent and are really hitting it off. It's like they have known each other all their life. They just click. This doesn't happen often in life. If you can find five people in a lifetime that you click with and are friends with for your entire life, you are blessed.

I read the poem to Kale and he loved it as much as Scottie did. Kale let all of us know that he also thought Bigfoot is a curious teenager. I liked hearing that.

Observing Scottie and Kale opened my eyes. They are so connected. Bigfoot brought them together, if not for him they would never have met and become friends. What I see before my eyes is a gift to both, Scottie and Kale, friendship.

Scottie, because he is very intelligent, has a difficult time making friends. Teens consider him to be weird, how sad that intelligence is labeled weird.

Kale has given Scottie a reason to come out of his shell and live life like it's meant to be lived. Friendship is powerful medicine. Kale asked if Scottie knew how to play chess. Scottie brought out the chessboard and the game began. Chess, in my opinion, demands a high level of intelligence. You must be able to focus and read the moves of your opponent before he even makes a move, you must be able to predict what he will do in the future. Not an easy task.

Scottie's mother asked Crystal and myself if we would like to watch a movie that was targeted at the female gender. She popped some popcorn and fixed us a fresh drink and we were good for two hours.

Just as the movie ended, Scottie and Kale walked into the room. Scottie said, "Sorry I was so rude, but seldom do I meet someone my age that knows how to play chess. Kale is a worthy opponent and we plan to finish our game tomorrow. Hope you ladies enjoyed the movie."

We all gave a thumb's up, and the conversation turned back onto Bigfoot. Scottie asked to look at the pictures of Bigfoot again and as we thumbed through the pictures, he came across the pictures of the blue butterflies. He held up the one picture that was a close up of the underside of the butterfly's wings that showed the legs and eyes of the butterfly. I thought it odd that Scottie held up my favorite picture, the one I plan to make a portrait of to hang on my bedroom wall. The Diva Girls plan was to have these pictures finished today but Bigfoot is such a distraction that our Diva leader Jan, told us to finish the project later.

Scottie and Kale studied the pictures of Bigfoot once again in detail and had lengthy conversations about each picture.

"Would you girls mind if I scanned your pictures of Bigfoot so I can have a hardcopy for myself and Kale. I think it would be nice if we were to leave pictures of Bigfoot that are laminated so the weather would not affect them, and leave them where you found the footprint. Also I want to leave my bat and baseball for him to play with. I hope you girls can escort Kale and myself to the spot where you found the footprint. Kale wants to leave his lunch box with some chips in it for Bigfoot. Do you girls have anything you want to leave for him besides hair bands and socks?" Scottie said.

Everyone got a chuckle out of what Scottie said about the hair bands and socks. I began searching my mind for what gift I will leave for Bigfoot. I don't know if our Bigfoot is a girl or a boy so it should not matter what I leave behind. I have some lavender perfume that Bigfoot would find interesting, and Crystal wants to leave her hairbrush.

What a good idea Scottie came up with, leaving a gift from each of us. I asked Scottie's mother to take a picture of the four of us so Bigfoot would know four teenagers left these gifts for him. I wonder what he will think when he sees a picture with Kale and Scottie in it. Will he hang it on the wall of the cave he lives in? I know he will feel connected to us and will treasure this picture forever after all we are all teenagers.

Excitement filled the air as we made plans for our march up the hill to leave Bigfoot a treasure box with gifts for him. We agree to meet in two days in the morning at Scottie's cabin. We need to arrange for the forest ranger to escort us up the mountain and to have all our gifts in order. By then it will be dry and we will not get all muddy.

The morning sun came crashing through our windows on the day of Bigfoot's party with gifts from all of us, and once again excitement filled my senses. Breakfast is in the air with the smell of bacon and eggs and orange juice. As I grabbed my tray, I scanned the room looking for Jan and Crystal. Jan is the first person I spotted so I make a V line for her table. I sit directly across from her and begin telling her of the plans for the day. I invite her to join us knowing her memory will be an asset to our once again discovering Bigfoot's path. You see animals and people alike have a tendency to take the same path regularly. Jan was thrilled to be asked and quickly found someone to take her place for all activities of the day with the Diva Girls.

Crystal spotted us and joined our table. I explained to Crystal that Jan would be joining us on our hike up Tiger Mountain today. Jan was still explaining the day's activities to her substitute who is sitting beside her.

"I have my hair brush and a little something extra, a new tooth brush still in the package. I hear Bigfoot has really bad breath, this should help," Crystal said.

"Great idea, although I think the problem with the smell is glands like the ones we have under our arms. It is a defense against harm. However, the toothbrush will help keep his teeth nice and white. Everyone likes shinny white teeth. By the way, Jan is joining us today, she will help us find where the footprint was," I said.

After we all finished our breakfast we headed for Scottie's cabin. Kale is already there and ready to start the hike. Scottie put out his hand and introduced himself to Jan. As they exchanged information about theirself the forest ranger arrived. He grabbed Jan's hand and said, "Welcome aboard Jan, the more the merrier." You see they already knew each other. This forest ranger was the leader for Kale's expedition. He is very excited to be joining us today. He brought colored pencils and drawing paper to leave for Bigfoot. Jan pulled out a mirror from her pocket to put in the box that the forest ranger was holding out. Crystal put her hairbrush and toothbrush in the box and I put in my lavender perfume. Kale put his lunchbox in and Scottie put pictures in, one is my favorite picture of the blue butterfly.

Scottie is going to carry his bat and ball. Soon his prize toys will belong to Bigfoot. He just wants to hold them as long as possible.

Off we went, up the hills of Tiger Mountain in search of the trail off the beaten path where we seen evidence of Bigfoot's existence.

The weather is a typical warm summer day and we are now near where we think Bigfoot left his footprint for us to find. We all feel he wanted us to see this footprint, because he is just to smart to make any mistakes.

"Over here, I broke this tree limb and left it attached to this very tree in case things went wrong somehow. This is the trail, follow me," Jan said.

Everything looked familiar, the thick brush that the footprint was beside and the boulder that I sat upon. Yes, this is the very spot that the footprint was made. We left our precious gifts in what was left of his footprint only now it is unrecognizable because he re-stepped on it. The forest ranger placed the box at the edge of the disturbed earth and Scottie placed his bat with the glove on the end of the footprint, against the boulder. We held hands and wished for Bigfoot to find the treasures we are leaving for him. We all feel a connection to Bigfoot especially Scottie, he feels Bigfoot was looking for a friend just like Scottie was when he met Kale. Friends must have something in common such as intelligence of equal value. If you don't have values to enhance your intelligence than you are just an intelligent human full of useless knowledge.

Since Kale and Scottie are extremely intelligent, is Bigfoot looking for a friend who is on his level of intelligence. Can Bigfoot sense how smart Scottie and Kale are? We can sense a person's greatness so why couldn't Bigfoot also have that ability. There is an old saying, 'Never be in the presence of greatness without acknowledgement of their greatness.' With our gifts we are trying to reach Bigfoot and let him know we think he is great.

As we began our way down Tiger Mountain the ground began to shake. My senses are so exaggerated that I'm aware of everything around me. I can smell the flowers before I see them, I can hear the birds before I see them, the silence at this moment is deafening. I can feel the silent intense energy in the ground below my feet. The ground suddenly burst open and between my feet is a crack in the earth. How could this happen, without a single sound. I could feel the air vibrating as if an out of body experience, everything is more intense and vivid. I focus on a leaf in front of my face and the light that is hitting it changes its color from green to gold to red. I'm watching the leaf to see if it moves, but only the color changes as the leaf remains as still as a mouse. There is a feeling of tranquility and freshness in the air, and my body feels weightless as I turn my head to look at the rest of my party. Everyone is as still as a statue with eyes as big as saucers. Thunder broke open the sky and a bolt of lightening jumped out of the crake of the earth. That's right, instead of the lightening coming from the sky it came out of the earth.

One and all we broke stride and headed down the mountain. Crystal yelled, "I'm going to get some yonder, this mountain is trembling and I can see the hills moving, run as fast as you can before the earth swallows us up. There is a dangerously fast moving crack in the earth heading our way."

I'm running as fast as I possible can and it is as if I can't get air into my lungs. The earth opened right in front of me and I'm looking into a glaring ball of fire. The eruption lasted for only a moment and the earth closed back up, as if nothing ever happened. Darkness filled the air as gray clouds fall on Tiger Mountain, a thought enters my mind 'I wonder what Bigfoot is doing right this very moment.'

When we made it to base camp it looked like nothing ever happened. I bent down and kissed the ground, I was so happy we made it. Jan gave everyone in the party a hug, and no words were spoken.

Professor Sprinkle greeted us and asked, "How bad was the storm up there? We didn't get a drop of rain down here, the dark clouds, loud thunder, and lightening up on Tiger Mountain looked frightening. We were fixing to put together a search party if you guys didn't show up pretty soon."

"We made it to our destination and left Bigfoot all his presents but on the way down there was an earthquake. Parts of the mountain opened up and I swear we were looking into the center of the earth. Fire and smoke began belching up one minute and the next minute it closed back up like it never even happened. It was mind boggling, what was going on up there. We were all overcome with astonishment and fright.

Do you remember when I talked about the earthquakes and sightings of Bigfoot seem to happen at the same time.

This is another incident where Bigfoot and earthquakes go hand in hand. Professor Sprinkle, Bigfoot knew about that earthquake days before it even happened," Kale said.

"It definitely was an earthquake, the boy is not exaggerating one bit about the earth opening up and fire being at the bottom of the pit we looked into. Tiger Mountain very well could turn into a volcano," said the forest ranger.

We all went back to Scottie's cabin and his mother met us at the door, "I'm so glad to see you guys, I've been worried sick about you. I called Professor Sprinkle and asked him to go up Tiger Mountain and bring you back down. It looked like a really bad storm was brewing up there," Scottie's mother said.

We told her the whole story about what happened while she fixed lunch and at times she turned white as a sheet, she must have thought about how we could of all been swallowed up in the crack of the earth, never to be seen again. She grabbed Scottie and just hugged him for a while.

The next day the camp was swarming with people who study geography, the study of the features of the earth. They interviewed each of us alone first, than as a group. I think they wanted to see if we all told the same story. The forest ranger escorted the group of geography experts up Tiger Mountain to show them where the earth opened up, they looked for evidence and found, ash, this is all the proof they needed. Ash, that only comes from a volcano.

The forest ranger visited the spot where we left Bigfoot's presents, and they were all gone. I image Bigfoot will always treasure our presents and I wonder if we will ever see him again. The pictures I took of the red dot in the trees on Tiger Mountain could not be proved to be or not to be Bigfoot. In my heart I will always know it was Bigfoot.

Scottie and Kale made a pack to always keep in contact with each other and be BFF's. Crystal and myself are comparing pictures of blue butterflies and deciding which ones we want to turn into picture's to hang on our walls.

This adventure will always be part of who I have become,

thanks to Bigfoot.   There is the one footprint Bigfoot left when he crossed over Scottie, it is proff enough that Bigfoot lives on Tiger Mountain.

The End

www.ingramcontent.com/pod-product-compliance
Lightning Source LLC
Chambersburg PA
CBHW021927170626
46807CB00007B/3011